CONTRACTS

P J Walters

First published in 2016

Waggledance Press, Blythe Bridge

Print ISBN: 978-0-9569668-2-7
E pub ISBN: 978-0-9569668-3-4

Waggledance Press

For Isolde P Roxby

INSIDE-OUT

With that I pull the window shut and I am inside. Bill draws away the ladder outside and pushes it quickly into the back of the van. Then he disappears back to the cab and suddenly I am alone. I'm also standing, lit yellow by the street lamps and framed perfectly by the window for any passerby to see, so I move back into the shadows and give myself a moment to gather my thoughts together.

The stairwell and landing feel much different in the dark, more like the soft light under a woodland canopy without the fluorescent strips. I go quietly downstairs and try the door. It's locked. Stillness has it, and silence, more so with every second as I strain to hear for signs of life inside. I climb back to the landing and up the stairs to the door that leads to the expanse of the hall on the other side. I know the layout well from the last time, when the exhibition space thronged with visitors. I listen for a moment and pull the door slowly, as if through custard, to make the least noise I can. Then I'm through and that much farther from Bill and the van.

The roof windows throw light pollution onto the expanse of the hall. This is the first floor. I will need to go into the unknown below to complete my task. I turn my camcorder on to night vision and take a panning shot, even though Bill and me and the other three have already seen this lot. I want to do this right.

'It'll be easy,' said Bill, 'Just take it easy, take your time, cover the ground and, when you're ready, back to the van.'

I wish my ears were younger. I crouch to listen, as if that makes things better, and take in the still quiet, even though we're not that far from the busy high street and traffic backwards-and-forwards in the night. I'm listening for signs: doors opening, footfall in the corridors, security rounds, but there's only my breath heaving in and out. Bill will have pulled the van away from the window somewhere out of sight. Breathing faster, telling myself there is no one else inside, getting to my feet and moving quickly along.

I am to proceed through as many rooms as I can, filming all the way and adding details of the layout to my plan. The purpose makes it possible to carry on. I go to the next door along from the one through which I have just entered. It says 'Private', but I open it and move inside: an office. Out with my pad and the preliminary sketch we already have: the main hall space, the entrance down the two sets of front steps with its ticket kiosk and gift outlet, the coffee shop right at the back, sundry sets of toilets, the rough outline of the offices and rooms down each side, the public lift, the one for goods and staff.

'Get it as much to scale as you can.'

I switch my headlight to its lowest setting and add doors and windows to the plan, quickly and quietly, and on to the next part, through interconnecting doors, feeling like I am being spotted by eagle-eyed passers-by all the time. Much too late I think that it would have been better to have dressed in a security outfit, blue jacket and strides with a peaked cap, rather than all in black like a villain with black thoughts on my mind. Sometimes I'm slow like that.

I don't want to spend too much time, but I want to get it right. I forget to look for the locations of cameras and work my way back – positions and angles. Some rooms are locked. Others lit by screen savers that make me lament the waste of power. Soon, I'm through one set of rooms and crossing the hall to the other side. It's simpler than we might have thought: one or two big office spaces, stationary cupboards, a little kitchenette, corporate items and personal items, the odd soft toy mascot, grey bins, in-trays and out-trays, rooms of files and executive spaces, the greater the workload, the smaller the personal space allowed.

I add what I can make out to my plan. It won't interest us too much, but we need to get as much information as we can. Information is everything in a heist. I move back to the hall. Once it was a manufactory and machine tools stood in rows from wall to wall, before the office partitions went up, when men were called to work by whistle and paid for honest toil. Now it's ghosts and the blood rushing in my ears as I make the first move towards the back of the hall and the unseen portions down the private stairs at the back.

It's dark downstairs and far less pretty than above, more like a cave. The space is a windowless expanse with a forest of cast-iron pillars holding up the first floor. It's littered with segments of exhibition stand and wooden pallets. There are wire cages towards the walls, staff toilets, telephone electronics and piles and piles of dusty boxes and redundant tat. I turn my head-torch to the highest setting and try and get a range of footage in night vision and daytime setting even in the low light. I direct the eye of the camera into every corner I can. I will get it all for Bill. We will have a three-dimensional map. I feel secure, because I can't be seen, and insecure because I'm so much further from the van. I can report the physical findings, but I can't relate quite how out of place this makes me feel, even for someone for whom out-of-placeness is a way of life.

I circulate. Right at the front extent there are locked doors leading to the entrance. At the back there is the service lift and an area which we have guessed, rightly, houses what one might call the security suite, were it not just two small rooms smelling of meat paste, coffee and bananas. So much for security: none of it is locked. I turn on the light and the glare leaches the visual purple from my receptors. There are two screens running, both showing the front lobby, five more turned off. I check quickly to see if I've been taped, but it's clear that there are no recording devices turned on. When we come back, no doubt that won't be the case, so we'll have to address that.

I sit for a minute and swivel nonchalantly in one of the chairs. I feel my momentum slacken. It's all too quiet and remote down in the dungeon. I know I have to go, but not quite yet. I know I have this job to do, that I'm going to do it for Bill, that I owe him that. At one point in my life I could have applied my free will, but not now. Free will means nothing when you have outlived your ambitions and desires. All that remains is to continue in some pattern of existence until all things come to an end, that, if you've got a job to do, then you give it your best and try not to let anyone down. That's all that's left. I rise from the seat and leave myself.

6

WAVERLEY

'How was it all?' Bill asks in the pub when I'm half way through my pint. We've been quiet in the van all the way back: I guess because he could sense me winding down.

'All good, I think I've got everything.'

'You'd better the fuck have, or you can go back in right now.' This is Mal. Euan has brought him. Deep, it seems has had to go off bouncing at short notice and is unavailable for our debriefing. We are meeting in the Waverley once again, even though somewhere less public might suit our delicate business somewhat better. I look directly at Mal, who has a good ten years on my forty, and wonder whether a stocky little miserabalist like him had to fight a lot when he was inside. I can just see him pissing people off at the drop of a hat. Not too bright. I bet Euan has committed ten times the offences, but he's never been off the streets. Perhaps time will tell: Euan's younger than me.

Bill is his usual, serene self or, if not serene, then not emotionally forthcoming, 'Calm this down, John will have it. We'll work it through back home. If there is anything else, then we'll take it from there.'

Bill has been Mal's boss for years, in legitimate business, so I know that there's going to be no contradiction. I can just sense that Mal feels like I've had a field promotion with this level of responsibility. And me the arriviste. I've barely been here a couple of months.

I don't much like the Waverley. Its romantic name sits uneasily with its 1960s modernist rough-cast construction and position amongst a sea of similar and charmless rough-cast houses. It's the kind of scene that only Scotland seems to be able to develop to this level of melancholy, a solid manifestation of the ever-present February drizzle. So far I've failed to voice my opinion, because I think that Bill was probably brought up here. All the boys seem at home in this environment. Then, Bill's far from out of place in his neo-Palladian country mansion. It's just me that's otherwise and, as Euan jabbers on about some shit in his broadest Lanarkshire accent, echoed many times over in the Thursday night pub crowd, I have another one of my sassenach moments and reach for the double Teachers that Bill has bought me to fortify my blood.

'What about the service doors?'

'You might know better, Mal, but I don't think we can do anything with them unless we can find the key for the shutter electrics. It's also padlocked to the floor.

'What sort of padlock?' He's trying to assert his expertise.

'One of those disc locks with a short rod.' I've been paying attention.

'Then we'll cut the staple.'

'The staple's covered by a thick box-work on the bottom rail of the door. There's just enough space to fit the padlock and rotate the bolt. As Bill says, there's the fire doors. They just push open. I could see the alarm sensors. I've got lots of footage. They don't look too sophisticated. You'll have to come up with an idea about that, won't you?'

Bill's serenity seems to me to float on a deep sea of tension. Things bother him through gritted teeth. Since I've got to know him better this time around it's easier to see what drives him. I wonder if Justine understands the personal cost.

Euan's up for the drinks: two heavies, a lager and a stout for me. I need building up. Even though I'm the tallest I feel a tad effete against the bouncer-boy physiques of Euan and Deep. When there are tasks ahead that are beyond your capabilities, you have to make yourself capable. Sometimes there are preparations; sometimes you make yourself able to do things simply by the act of doing them.

In the morning I'm tired but strangely elated. I fell asleep saturated with stout without registering that I hadn't had anything to eat. My flat in the garage isn't too warm. There are only a couple of storage heaters and they don't do much against the Scottish weather. It's been grey and wet since Christmas. Bill, Justine and Lauren will be snug up at the main house with its state-of-the-art underfloor heating. I am in Bill's orbit, fifty metres out, drawn into his gravitational field. Moons like me are subject and orbits derive from a constant breaking away and being held back, leading to a predictable ellipse, round and round until the heavens collapse.

Mornings are the same with me: coffee is followed by teeth cleaning – they don't work the other way round. I won't see anyone until I have to, which might be too soon if I'm driving Lauren to school. Bill usually lets me know the night before.

I make what I can to eat in the kitchen side of the living room. I can never eat too early – my system doesn't like it. The best I can manage is elevenses. Today I am hung over, which means I won't eat until lunch.

In my small and outdated apartment I listen only to classical music or silence. There is a TV, but no aerial. If I watch anything it will be DVDs – preferably from America or anywhere where I have no personal history. The same thing goes for books: nothing from the canon or contemporary fiction, just foreign crime noir, fantasy and science fiction, far-off worlds from California to Ultima Thule.

Sometimes Bill has things for us to do. Having stuff to do helps keep out the worst images in my head. I try to live solely in thc now. There is no joy in thinking about my past, so I block it out as much as I can. Anything that happened more than a couple of years ago is now so distant to me that it happened to someone else. I have no connections left except for Bill. Imagining that I have is fruitless.

I open the door and look out into the garage. I'm up a flight of stairs that leads down onto the garage floor. It's more a motor house really, with space for four cars in a square and a long workbench running down one side. It dates from the Thirties, I think. The house that went with the garage is now knocked down and Bill's house-for-the-aspirant built in its place. The grounds in which the whole lot stands runs to perhaps two acres. The garage is away from, and below the house. I am away from, and below, Bill's family. But it's something in a world of nothing. The garage is two steps colder even than the cold flat and it's not time for my exercises, so I step back inside and close the door. Perhaps there might be enough hot water for a bath. With no word from Bill I have an empty day ahead.

In the event I am up at the house by mid day. Bill wants to work through the camcorder stuff and collate it with the plan. Even though I'm safe in his living room, something of last night's atmosphere comes back. I read into the green images the presence of myself, or an avatar self, reliving the excitement and fear. Bill asks questions like, 'Where's this on the plan?' and 'Which door is that?' He wants to know exactly which are locked and what I think might be behind them. We redraw the plan more neatly on a bigger sheet and review the sight-lines that we have established exist outside the building. There is further footage of that. There are still pictures. There's a tenth generation blueprint of the premises when it was still a factory, though it doesn't tell us anything worth knowing. Bill asks more questions – details, details, details. He's trying to create a template in his mind.

And he's not even the thief. Mal is the one who's done time for housebreaking. It was some time ago, but I get the impression he did it for a living. Bill is a businessman, even if business hasn't been entirely on the legal side. This venture is something of a departure, but Bill doesn't seem to think he has a choice. I've noticed that he's dogged when there's some task he's about. Even today there are no breaks, because he wants to get packed away before Lauren and Justine get back. He works it through in a methodical way, which I like. The others haven't got the nous for that – Mal hasn't the sparkle, Deep and Euan are just bouncers who don't mind a little extra-curricular activity and deal drugs on side. Bill will hold it together.

'How's it feel?' he says.

'Feel?'

'What feeling do you get? How easy is it going to be to get around inside?'

'You know, it's not really my field.' But I have been inside places before when I shouldn't have been. 'It's one thing when it's empty, but it might be different when it's full. They might lock some doors and unlock others. What we've come up with so far looks right as far as I can tell. You should ask Mal.'

'Mal was just a common burglar. I don't credit him with much. That's why you went inside, because we need someone who can think their way through a problem. He can shift boxes, he's good on the mechanics of a prophylactic machine, there are other things that might figure as we get on. From you, I want to know what you feel.'

I don't feel much these days. 'Feels all right, but it's just an empty shed right now. We need to look at how it is once the exhibition's underway.'

Bill goes to the cabinet and fills a couple of glasses with scotch. He has all kinds of drinks in there. If I have a drink at my place I tend not to stop until it's gone, however long it takes. I ration myself because of that and because there's a psychological toll to pay. I've been like that since the end of my last job barely two years back. On The Route the money I made was good, but the costs astronomical.

'Thanks.' I sip, because it's still just mid afternoon. Even so, the northern sun has gone down in the west and there arrives another cold and damp night, just like every night.

Lauren is on the tall side of medium height. At eighteen she's already passed Justine. It could be that she'll put on another spurt, but I think that she's probably done. She has fully formed, with dark hair and pale blue gems for eyes. She has a directness that comes from never having been set back on the path of life, which makes me sad, because I know of the pain that will inevitably come. Now, she is a spring leaf unhardened by the summer sun. She is a creation of winter, an ice princess, though hardly as quiet. She arrives a little after four with Yvonne, who is staying for tea. Justine knows about this, even if Bill doesn't. Justine is slightly delayed by her job at the optician's. Yvonne's dad has brought them back. His house is another like this one, only closer to the golf course and with half the grounds. I've been there dropping Lauren off, though not inside.

'We're going to do some studying for our exams after tea,' she says, with a conspirational giggle that suggests something more entertaining. Young people have endless outlets to keep them occupied these days. They have more electronics in their rooms than the BBC. 'We're going to have a snack, do you want anything?'

'Not just now, hen.'

The question did not include me. I take Lauren to school, I bring her back, but Bill doesn't quite like me to mix too much with the family. It's nothing personal, something more to do with the measures I represent. Justine and Lauren are the good side; I am the bad. I don't think that he's conscious of it, only he wants to keep his family protected from that. I'm not strictly someonc in any case, more like a garden gnome or pet banished to the outside.

Yvonne is pretty too, though her eyes are brown, I think. I drive these girls around while they giggle in the back, interrupted by interludes of maturity and bouts of questions that I’m unable to answer. What to think of all that? I can’t make out. I give little of myself away. Easy, because I’m not myself. I don’t even have a real name.

MOBILE

Bill's works is empty now, save for those precious few boxes of prophylactics that are required for trade and the shells and guts of half a dozen chewing gum machines with names like *Beech Nut* on them in faded paint. Spider webs have softened the intersections of the shelves and a skin has formed on the water of the men's toilet downstairs.

Bill, I know, feels the loss of the stuff I used to deliver when I was plying The Route. It was profitable, clearly, and would have made all the difference, bearing in mind the slow-down in the family-planning business. The way The Route collapsed so quickly would have left him rapidly out in the cold. You can't legislate for things like that, and there's no comeback.

The works is not unlike my garage. I guess it's from a similar period. There's a yard outside, big doors and a loading bay, a warehouse floor and open stairs up to a suite of offices. When The Route was still operational it was a busy place to turn up to, with half a dozen employees downstairs and two secretaries and Bill upstairs. That's all gone now. The business was undercut by the multinationals and the increasing number of fakes. 'They look just right,' said Bill, 'but they're not right. Who knows what they're using for spermicidal lubricant and some of them have fucking holes in. What's the point of that?'

Everything is fake: the cheap bulk condoms that have undercut Bill's business, DVD's that haven't even been officially released, cats' piss perfume in brand-identical packaging, all kinds of medication for the sub-priapic, designer watches, all the sports clothing labels and every size and variation of every item in their range. I'm not even genuine myself.

Euan's evangelical about it. 'There's not enough money selling handfuls of drugs anymore. I know a guy who can get hundreds of pairs of knock-off Nikes at two pounds a pair. Thousands if you want. What can you sell those for? Twenty pounds a pair? That's a hundred percent profit.' (maths isn't a strong point, though his eyes light up when he talks about money). 'Now then, how about your Louis Vuitton? Just a fucking shopping bag and it's a thousand pound – buy them for fifty; sell them for three hundred.'

It's Saturday and we've just loaded the phones for the last time. I backed up to the load bay and docked neatly in the aperture. The never-opened boxes passed like gametes from the body of the works to the womb of the van. Bill was quiet throughout. He would rather be with his family and the phones have been the only thing keeping his finances going. I've lost count of the times we've shifted them round. I know that he's regretted not being able to have invested more in the scheme, but so much now is tied up in the house. The works is mortgaged to the hilt and is standing idle. The phones were the only thing of any worth in it. Now they're in the van and onto their last spin on the carousel. I don't think it's too bad in one sense: nothing goes out of fashion faster than a mobile. Something about the VAT rules has changed as well, so we can't keep hiving it off, re-invoicing and moving on. He's made enough even with insufficient stock and it would be stupid to draw attention from the authorities when we have other fish to fry.

It's incredible how I've missed driving over these two years. In all that time I didn't have a sniff of a bike seat or a steering wheel beneath my fingers. When The Route collapsed I left the old sports bike outside my abandoned flat. I wonder how long it lasted before it was gone. Not too long, I think, with the keys left in the ignition. I just dumped my old white van, right after my final trip. Then it's been public transport all the way and I don't like that.

We spin along the M8 towards Edinburgh, tightening our central belts in the face of recession. I'm driving. The phones lie innocently in the back, unaware of their fraudulent past. When I think about it, I haven't delivered anything legitimate since I worked riding for despatch, sometime in a another universe in another life. How easy it is to accommodate yourself to sliding standards when you've convinced yourself that there's no choice.

Perhaps, for Bill, I've pitched up at the right time. I've only been here a couple of months and already I'm knee deep in the operation. Perhaps he needs someone to be in it with him or maybe just someone to drive. I don't ask too many questions about that, but then the boys aren't the ultimate company, even if they're more than willing. Maybe Bill sees that I have nothing and having something is what I need. Maybe he's a natural sort of boss and I'm a natural kind of employee. Anyway, I drive well, it's a point of pride and, even though the M8 amidst the dreich might not be pinnacle of travel, it's better than sitting alone at home gradually digesting oneself.

He's still thinking about the plan.

'If we use the exit we're planning, what are we going to do about the steps?' I ask.

'I'm not done with that.'

'But you think we can work it?'

He grunts something that I take to be an affirmative. He wants to ponder, not talk. So I drive eastwards and settle into the rhythm.

We're nearing Edinburgh, so Bill relays instructions from the sat nav he's brought from the Audi. It's all quite straightforward, except that the property we're delivering to is a big terraced house near Corstorphine with double yellow lines outside. Normally I would never park up in a van at a restricted spot, but I'm not the boss. Bill goes off and speaks to a guy at the door while I watch out for traffic wardens and cops.

We have to unload the whole lot ourselves while the two purchasers watch. It's just like the old days when I delivered the Stuff: barely a kind word and everyone tense and agitated. There are many boxes of phones, almost too many for the van, and the drizzle makes a mountain out of the job. Bill finds the paperwork and goes off into the house while I wait to get a parking ticket, but the traffic gods seem to be looking favourably on me today and we get off free. Bill's even less happy now that the phones have finally gone for good. I know he's already been paid and I guess that the money's already spoken for. I'm not too happy because I just have to turn round and retread my route, also that, once the job has finished, the long evening will stretch ahead with me alone in my flat.

I look out for the features of the outward bound journey to divide up the time going back: Bathgate; Whitburn. Bill is still quiet. Why has he taken me so far into his confidence when Mal would be a more logical option? Or Deep? Or Euan? Because they're not as bright as they think they are, even if they do possess a kind of criminal cunning that can spot the opportunities for a fast buck. I have never thought like that, I can just obviate my conscience when there's money to be had.

By the time we get back to the works it's, once again, dark. The days are brief this time of year. They get started just in time to stop. I park up in the yard and follow Bill into the works. By rights we should be taking the Audi and getting back to the house. Instead, we turn on the lights and go up to the office, sit and wait. Deep turns up in his doorman outfit. Apparently, Bill doesn't let me in on everything.

Deep is something of a gymnasium monster. His given name is Deepak, but he's never called that. He's maybe four inches shorter than me and four inches wider. His suit's still quite sharp and he's not one of those body builders with unsightly bulges. He has something in an envelope for Bill.

'What happened to you?' He's seen the cut above Deep's eyebrow.

'Bit of a fight.'

'Yeah?'

'With some guy at the Starz.'

Starz is one of the night clubs that Euan and Deep work for, although it sounds more like 'stairs' the way they say it.

'Unhappy punter, eh?'

'Not this time, it was one of Osman's mob.'

I've heard this name before. I'm not even sure it's a real name, just some all-purpose Johnny-foreign moniker. In the course of conversation the Osmans have been variously referred to as Albanian, Turkish, Polish, Lithuanian, Latvian and everything else slightly beyond the borders of knowability. I know that they have been implicated in all kinds of activities, including the marketing of fake condoms, which is why Bill is looking unhappy at the mention of the name. It's a little tight-knit here, and I feel wee filigree hintets of prejudice coming from some quarters, like incomers might be a bad idea and that, without anyone noticing, they've managed to infiltrate themselves into everywhere and everything.

Of course, Euan has something to say on that, 'They're like a fucking virus. They're not scared of anyone. They move in and they take over the sex trade. They've got themselves nice wee suburban semis with half a dozen working girls doing shifts twenty-four seven. You can get yourself sucked off for twenty and the lot for fifty, all foreign girls, don't speak Scottish, fourteen and fifteen year old wains, but pretty, straight off the boat. They've got a boss that runs three or four houses and they're all related, brothers and cousins from the same village somewhere. Then there's protection money and cheap drugs, blow, speed, poppers. Osman creams off the top. He's the big fucking boss…'

And so on and so on. Bill offers Deep a drink, but he refuses. He never drinks when he's working on the door, only afterwards.

'What about, then?'

Deep gives the dried cut a little rub. 'Some guy called Atil. He was trying to sell drugs in *my* club. We don't stand for that. We control the door, we control the trade. It's that simple. He knew that, I've seen him around, but he didn't want to take no for an answer.'

'So he chinned you?'

'That was just an incidental, he didn't come out of it too well.'

‘You want to watch it, they’ll put a contract out on you’

‘Fuck 'em, fuck the little cunt, he knew what he was doing, he paid the price, fuck him and all the rest of them. Anyway, I’ve got to be off – I don’t want to be late.’

With that he straightens his tie and leaves. Bill picks up the envelope and rises. Time for home, one more endless night and another solitary meal.

SUNDAY

I no longer have a past as such. The past exists only as a place to have come from, an old country with old customs that have now been set aside. You had a name there now fallen into disuse and forgotten. When you used think about the past it was the same as your infant imagination trying to conceive what there was beyond the bounds of the universe: after covering the same ground countless times without answers you just stopped going there.

How does it come about, that despite your best efforts, you wash up in a situation where your life has been threatened and you have lost contact with everything and everyone that made you a place in the world?

I no longer have a future as such. This has been the case longer, even, than lacking a past. The two now press respectively from behind and ahead, squeezing the present into a thin sliver of current existence, ticking along at sixty seconds a minute, sixty minutes an hour. In this tiny vessel I move from moment to moment, almost weightless, with the giant weight of the world resting painfully on my shoulders, struggling forwards just to continue to exist. In this state there is no capacity to carry anything or anyone else with you. Even when there are others around, you are completely alone.

I can never again have any connection with anyone I've ever known or cared about, just in case there is danger. In these two years I've never been certain that there is anyone looking for me, but one way or another it's always felt like there is. I don't think it really matters. There's so little about me now, that I've expired in all but fact. Family, friends, such as they are, places and artefacts, have all been left in calmer waters far behind.

Each minute lasts sixty seconds, each second evaporates in the hand before it is registered or realised, the next one comes up and dies in turn. Each instant leaves infinitesimal marks on the surface of your skin. With time the marks accumulate until they become visible, growing at an imperceptible rate until they form scars. The more time, the more scars; the greater the distance from which they can be seen.

Time stops when the scars work deep enough into your system to halt the mechanism that drives you.

Living in the continuing moment denies you any conception of other possibilities. It is your lot just to be and do. Having a task helps with that. When the tasks are at an end, that's when the trouble starts. Stuck in the moment, one may be moving along with time, but there's no potential for personal growth or change. Yet, on some level, I still seem to want to go on.

Rain pours over the corrugated roof of the garage. Sunday is the worst day because there is rarely any activity on the agenda. Bill has taken Justine and Lauren out in the Audi. Justine's Mini remains, but I'm not permitted to drive that. The house is away from any village and all public transport routes. Going for a walk would be negatively edifying, so the only thing left to do is to swing on the bars.

The roof structure of the garage is supported on six 'A' frames over the parking area, made from steel tube in various diameters. The roof has quite a high pitch and the frames form broad-based triangles. There is a long cross-beam at the bottom, a lesser one about half way up and a small one just beneath the apex. Extra triangulations link these up and strengthen them, making comprehensive frames.

The game consists of getting up onto the work bench and getting hold of lowest cross beam of the first frame. From the moment that I pull myself up I must not touch the ground. There is a pattern of motion to observe: firstly, to traverse the width of the garage on the lower beam, to work back to the middle and then to escalate to the middle bar and left and right along that. Finally, to get to the top beam and then back down. From this lower beam I can then swing onto the next frame along and repeat the exercise, though it's something of a stretch. When you first start this kind of thing, it's all you can do to hold on for a few seconds before you have to let go, but gradually you can build up the strength in your arms. I have a kitchen timer set up on the bench. To start I set myself two minutes, then two and a half and so on until I could finish the whole routine on one frame. Then I left behind the timer and started counting frames. So far I am up to two and a half. Today I will try for three whole frames before I have to give up. I may not use my legs to help get from one level to the next and my feet must not touch the ground at any time or that effort is disqualified. This is my sole discipline in life.

This is how you pass the time in the prison you've made for yourself. Does spring ever come to this place? All is the endless drizzle of the northern winter and an unsubstantiated myth that there may one day be blue skies. Only change demonstrates the passage of time. When the weather remains unchanged, who is to say that there is any chronology? We go to sleep and wake again in the same day, to relive it again, wearing ourselves down with the repetition, the grey sky stays silent and the trees look dark and flat against the fading light, reminding us that we were once green and flexible like children. Now our sap has withdrawn to the root and our extremities dry out and become fragile in the wind. We bolster ourselves against winter storms and try to brave the onrush of the gale like good soldiers in the face of the enemy.

I will stop reading, I think. Crime novels become meaningless when you are living in one; science fiction and fantasy make my own world seem inadequate. I will watch films to occupy me, even if it means three a night.

I almost manage three frames, but I haven't got the gumption to make it right to the top. Sometimes you make good progress; sometimes you don't. I wonder how the boys would do, who seem to have won bulk by some genetic advantage and worked it up to its logical conclusion. Best to use yourself as your own bench mark. Hopefully, you make yourself tired enough to sleep though the night without constantly waking. Maybe you stave off a little of the ageing process and, definitely, you've used up a small portion of the day.

PLANNING

There are many stages in the prosecution of a crime. At least the sort that we're planning. Dillinger had it right, planning and rehearsing the moves in a military fashion, so that the actual event is simply a practical run-through of established patterns.

First, you have to have your big idea or establishing concept. For us, or really for Bill, this is *We will rob the Exhibition*. Why? Because there are things we want to possess. Why? Because we hope to improve our position in the state of the world. In Bill's case it means he can keep his house and look after his family to the standard to which he has aspired. How? This is the question. In fact it's hundreds of questions rolled into one. Many will have to be answered to the full on this tack; others probably can't be answered with any degree of certainty. This will lead to the random element or 'chance'. Chance has to be reduced to the lowest possible level to maximise the potential for a successful outcome. How to achieve this? Meticulous preparation and planning.

Bill has some military background. I think that this is where he met my old boss, Terence. He has never spoken about it and I have never asked. I don't suppose that either of them had long or glittering careers and I don't think that Bill is necessarily a master of strategy, but he is systematic. Indeed, his level of application to any given task is exemplary. But he doesn't go a bundle on subtlety. None of them do. Perhaps that's where I come in. I may not be much of a self-starter, but I'll do nuance and fine detail 'til the cows come in. I have my place on the team. With Bill, my presence forms a contract. He has taken me in and put a roof over my head. He passes me a little cash – enough to keep me ticking over. In return I pledge my labour to his task. If I fulfil my contract, I will receive reward.

So far we have talked up the job at endless meetings in the Waverley and at the works, fine-tuning the range of our questions. In a boundless field, those questions can become innumerable, so the first step is to set your parameters. Then your research can be confined to what is really significant. There is a balance: getting enough information to do the job, without getting bogged down in a data-sea of mud.

The concept is sound, because people steal stuff all the time and get away with it. Different venues have different levels of security. The exhibition hall will have valuable exhibits from time to time, but it's not a bank vault. It will have weaknesses. If there are valuables to be had, then reason says that getting possession of them is best accomplished when they are least secure. Logic suggests that this is when they are in transit, but the practical aspects outweigh the logic: Will there be Police escort? Maybe not, but there may be other forms of protection. Can we find out times and routes? Not without inside assistance and that's not likely to be forthcoming. If we could find out, could we pull off a hold-up on public roads? Bill and the younger members of the team no doubt have the beads for it, but is this sort of full-blooded gambit the type of project for a start-up operation like ours? Probably not. So, by and by, we decide to continue our task by methods of stealth, at least right up until the final moments. We talk and debate and tell stories about what we've seen and heard other people do. Deep refers too much to stuff he's seen on TV and on films, we rein him back to sober realities, even as we pile on the alcohol to fuel our discussions. After time we have covered all the theory and it's time for practicalities. First off, we have to get a look at the hall from the outside.

We went in different combinations, usually at night. Mal was mostly interested in the building. For a thick shit he seemed to have a remarkably good grasp of the physical attributes of doors and windows, ease of access, the comparative security of locks and catches, security cameras, where the quiet places might be. Bill was more concerned with the layout of the surrounding roads, street lights, one-ways, fast routes in, fast routes out, access for vehicles, peak pedestrian and traffic times. I could help with this, using knowledge from my despatch days: nothing makes you more aware of road conditions then the vulnerability of being on a bike amidst the high pressures of the courier life. Deep and Euan didn't get much further than a quick butcher's at the front entrance and coming up with a smash-and-grab ram-raid scheme. Mal took the piss out of them in the debrief afterwards. What about the steps up to the front? How were they going to keep momentum up the steps and still punch through all the steel and safety glass with no run up? What were they going to do about the Police security camera with its excellent view of the entire frontage? What the fuck were Deep and Euan for, exactly?

We'd taken notes, got pictures, planned it all on paper, looked at it enough times, then we moved on to the next stage. Finalising the external picture sets up your theatre of operations; getting inside refines the picture.

We entered the exhibition hall independently. I'd wondered whether baseball caps and shades might have been the order of the day, but Mal seemed to think that it didn't matter, 'No one fucking looks; no one fucking cares. How many people are going through the door today?'

Lots – I'd suggested the computer fair rather than the fine art exhibition for that very reason: a torrent versus a trickle. Also, I wouldn't get distracted by the art and give myself away as an aesthete when I was supposed to be casing the joint. The fair was also just a two day thing, so we figured a greater potential for throughput chaos and concealment. Deep wasn't available, so it was just the four of us. The fewer the better, I thought.

Rain made the townscape smell more grey than it actually was, rain with soot particles from coal fires and combustion engines. Mal wanted in first, so we let him go to get rid of him. Euan was wearing some posh suede jacket that didn't want getting wet, so he went soon afterwards. This left Bill and I hovering in doorways on opposites sides of the main shopping street trying to look independent with the same agenda. My shoulders trembled with more than cold. Ever since Bill told me about the job I've been feeling short of the right stuff. I'm more of your underexposed criminal – delivering contraband quietly in a van is one thing, breaking and entering is another. It's too much exposure, too much like real criminality. It's harder to square with yourself.

He'd told me about the plan just before our first group meeting at the works. For weeks I'd been doing odd jobs hanging around with Bill. Sometimes we'd clean the years' accumulation of detritus from the wound-down prophylactic business out to the tip, bits of machinery, boxes, paperwork and flyers, stickers, thousands of out-of-date rubber Johnnies, each one a sexual encounter that would never now happen.

At other times I'd drive him around, or drive Lauren. Occasionally we'd motivate the phones on another round of the carousel, but always Bill seemed restless, like he'd lost an empire and failed to find a role, constantly looking towards a metaphorical horizon for the next thing, all the time fretting on some deep level about the failing finances. With him I tended not to say much or to ask, unless it was about the wheres and whats of the job in hand.

Meetings took place always in the empty secretaries' office when they were at the works. Mal I'd met from one or two of the big instances of clearing out. Euan and Deep were new. Bill intimated that they had been part of the distribution chain for the stuff I used to deliver wholesale. That seemed about right, based on my own meagre experience. One was always just a small link in the chain and knew all one had to know and no more.

When Euan walked in that first time, he took one look and me and said, 'Who's this?' with the air of someone who has stumbled across an unexpected turd.

'He's John, he's with me,' said Bill, evidently not fazed by the marked tone of hostility. In criminal spheres no one likes an unknown or unannounced geezer. You need to come with a recommendation from a respected party and/or unimpeachable bona fides. I'm sure that Bill has told them nothing about my part in the last scheme. I don't come with any stories and they don't like that. They all have their stories. Euan's banged on about his killer deal selling on two stolen Mercs during the rise of the Russian oligarchs – 'They were out of the country within twenty-four hours and no paper trail. All cash in a kiddies' rucksack. Fucking profit all the way.'

Mal harks back to his scams on the building game. 'We were doing a redevelopment at a big factory and we came back at night and took the copper. We got hold of a JCB – you can start some of them with a coin. There was a big underground electricity supply running from a substation to a plant room, two hundred yards of thick armoured cable. We hitched an end up to the digger and dragged it all back out of the ground, tearing up the tarmac as we went. Thing is [and he pauses here and laughs] it took up everything else as well, the fucking water main, sewage, gas, the lot. What a fucking mess! We had it away so fast, and in the company flat bed. Three of us went to Lanzarote on that, three star hotel and all the pish you can drink.'

I pictured a litany of company power tools passing through Mal's hands, sold on in pub car parks for a fraction of their value.

Deep was a little less aggressive when he turned up. Once he'd established that I was some old fucker who wasn't in the same kind of gym-toned shape that he was, I was evidently no kind of threat and he was easy going. I could tell straight away that he was a bouncer – I've done business with them. Euan wasn't so easy to decode. He looked like a bouncer, but without all the attitude. For him, his door jobs are part of a social milieu that permits a certain type of commerce: you need access to punters who want to get pissed all night, forego all judgement and pay inordinate amounts for recreational substances.

None of the boys have an iota of respect for the proprieties of ownership; ownership is possession, all one needs to do is find the means to possess. Every moment of their waking day is analysed for avenues of gain from whatever angle. They're not clever people in the academic sense, but they have a keen vision that will find the slightest potential for graft in any given situation.

Bill just does business, but then he's a subtly different kind of animal. He looks at the bigger picture and proceeds whether the road is legitimate or not.

Yet none of these people do I think about as bad men: Deep's vain and self-serving, Euan has portable morals and Mal's a tosser, but I don't think I detect the whiff of evil about them. They're not sociopaths or mindlessly violent, their actions are predicated on the situations in which they find themselves. If those situations most readily suggest sub-legal actions, then so be it.

They know I don't fit in, but it's easily got round. I don't tell stories and I don't come with a history. But Bill's in charge so it's a done deal. When we drink I drink as much as them. I never miss a round and I'm not lax when my turn comes about. At meetings I drink like a Scotsman: I've had lots of practice.

When we were all together that first time, and some way through the first bottle of Teachers, Bill passed round the brochures – *A new exhibition: Art and Execution.* There were glossy pictures of the forthcoming exhibits: painting and sculpture, ceramics, cad-cam, disc production, printing, jewellery, with jewellers working live on items throughout the show.

'They're gems,' said Mal, 'they'll be fucking nailed down tight. What are you thinking, man?'

So Bill set to and told us.

I go into the hall after Euan, because I guess that Bill wants to see it done. It occurs to me that we have all waited just the right amount of time to look innocent and, hence, similar enough intervals to look suspicious. Perhaps the others can manage to look nonchalant on command, but I cannot. As soon as I am through the big glass doors and into the atrium I am at a loss. I am aware that all the everyday people here know what they have come to and have no questions about browsing the stores looking at software and computer parts. I am here to search for weaknesses, so my whole demeanour is wrong from the outset. So I stand there for an immortal age twiddling my mental thumbs, proceeding nowhere, feeling that the eyes of every available member of staff have already picked me out for a villain. I can feel the pained expression on my face. My body has become stiff and hard to move. I envy the unaffected crowds passing around me, making their way to the staircases that lead up to the exhibition space. I ponder the intricacies of their orthodox lifestyles, their habits, pastimes, desires and longings. I read alternative histories for myself, knowing that nothing now is possible and the only thing to play for is the job in hand. Everything is a nightmare and the dream happens somewhere else, seen though a fish tank. And then I have to move, because Bill will be coming in behind me if I hang around too long. *It's a public space*, I tell myself, *You are an approximation of a member of the public, get on with public activities.*

It's packed upstairs. We've selected a time soon enough after opening that the bargain hunters will have gathered together at the altar of consumerism and many of the more laid back will have arrived. Stalls are lined up in the manner of a medieval market, up-and-down rows piled with thousands of software titles, motherboards, cases, keyboards and peripherals, speakers, modems and power supplies, plain cardboard boxes bearing the familiar sans serif typefaces the Chinese use for export goods. I feign interest as best I can. It's all so mundane that my self-consciousness begins to slip away. It's warm inside after the rain. The feeling of exposure is less pronounced bumping into assorted types looking at products rather than their direction of travel. Most are men and boys, with the odd bored-looking woman. I always look for the women. Why is that? I play a game, seeking out the elusive nerd girls who have come because they wanted to. Maybe I'm being sexist, thinking that it's all boys' toys. A fine looking woman in a trouser suit walks by. Her badge tells me she's staff. Soon we will rob you. You don't know me and you never will. You didn't even see me when you sailed by.

It's clear, now that I am inside, that the exhibition space doesn't extend as far as the walls on either side or to the back. There are rooms. Some doors are evidently public access and some are not. I formulate a path to get me around enough to see everything. We need to know every inch of this space if we are to move effectively through it when the time comes, when we make it our own.

Above me the ceiling is pitched with a glass apex like that of a Victorian station running the full length. I imagine us abseiling down on black ropes from a cut-out section, but only in a Bond film. The drop is maybe thirty feet. I look at each door, trying not to bump into people now that I'm distracted on my own account. I make myself small so that I'm not noticed. I walk past Mal, who makes an issue of deliberately looking away. I get distracted by some computer art. I feel thirsty. I need a piss. The mechanisms of my sorry existence continue regardless. I lose track of time. I'm tired. I was too wound up earlier and it's drained me. I want a strong drink, but I make do with a coffee and a bun at the café at the back of the hall. Bill sits down behind me. We're back to back.

'Mal's found something.'

I thought we were supposed to remain out of contact. Our phones are switched off. We don't know each other. 'What?'

'The stairwell behind the third door on the right hand side. The big arched window on the landing halfway down. It's not alarmed. He says it's easy. Take a look.'

I don't answer. Then Bill might not have been talking to me. I get a feel for things quickly. If I wasn't adaptable I would never have been able to get myself into this shit in the first place.

As it is, the door is one of those marked 'Staff Only.' I have to get in unseen with a thousand eyes available to see me. I can picture Mal striding through with a 'Sorry, pal, I didn't ken it was private. I was just looking for the bogs.' I'm far too self aware for that kind of approach, even if I could lie for England.

At my first attempt someone is coming up the stairs and I have to get back through to the public space super-quick. That old apprehension has returned, but now my body feels light and limber. I wait until the guy in overalls has disappeared from sight and I'm through instantly. A short flight of stairs lead down to a landing that turns left and to the rest of the stairs down to who-knows-where? This is just a stairwell. There are no other doors. On the landing a wide arch of window lets in light. I can see from here that the top half opens and that there is a central catch. A thought, but there is no CCTV in here. For a moment I am my own master. I descend slowly to the window and take my time checking it out, every millimetre. There are no wires, no locks and just one rotary latch in the middle. It is in the unlocked position.

Deep met us at the Waverley later. Mal was in his element, his little bit of status. Euan toyed with some electronic organiser gizmo he'd bought at the fair.

'I hope you didn't pay for that on credit.'

'Fuck it, Mal, who's going to know? We all went through CCTV on the way through anyway.'

Bill looked straight at Euan, 'Let's keep to business. Mal?'

'This. There's no alarm on that widow – definitely not. There's just the one catch and I pushed it back. The window goes wide open and it's low enough to the outside to get a man up and through with a short ladder. It's way off the main street and out of the way of cameras.'

The window had looked dark and forbidding when we'd seen it from the outside during earlier reconnaissance. Now it seemed like a gift.

'This is next,' said Mal, 'I reckon they're not too hot on security. Someone should go back tomorrow and see if the catch is still open.'

'Who?'

'Me. I'll go in the afternoon when they've had the night and day to find it and close it. If not, we're in.'

'And then?'

'Then? Then I reckon we get in when it's quiet and have a proper look around.'

'That's what I've planned. The next exhibition is in eight days. The computer fair runs down tomorrow, so Mal will go in and check the window. After that they'll be building up for the fine art thing. That runs for two weeks. If we give them two days to clear up afterwards, then we can put our man in. *Art and Execution* is the week after that and they might well start to set up for that. I reckon that we might have a window of a couple of days between breaking down and setting up.'

We stayed quiet for a moment

'The one who goes in will make a detailed plan of the layout and security measures. We want to know everything inside-out before we go in proper, because I'm not anxious to risk my liberty.'

Mal nodded, 'All right, but you're going to have to give me plenty of time inside.'

'You're not going in, John is.'

'Why John?' said Euan.

'Because he's the one with an education and he'll do the job that I want doing.'

How does he know about my education? I've never told him.

DRIVE

In this season time is dormant. No change but the idle preamble of snowdrops hoping to struggle from the ground. Ambition sleeps. Winter rules in a totalitarian way, without quarter. Each aspect of existence feels like it has sunk to the lowest common denominator. It is said in some cultures that lack of change is the very nature of death. No life, no change. In these endless months of northern winter, cold and wet to the touch, we rub through, resisting abrasions of frost and ice, leaving raw skin and chapped lips. Our eyes water not out of pity for ourselves, but because the wind brings forth tears. Beneath the ground we harbour frayed nerves, hoping to make it through to another spring, keeping all things on hold, don't rush into anything... *too late*.

I'm up especially early to take Lauren to school. I like this even though I'm not great early on: it takes too much effort. Lauren is tired from homework, she says, but it doesn't show. I have to collect, also, Yvonne and Kirsty. Yvonne's dad has already gone to work. He's a property developer, I'm told. Yvonne's mother stays at home or spends time shopping or fills in time with her friends. I haven't been told this, I just know. Yvonne's mother doesn't like the look of me very much. I'm not surprised: I'm the toad in the driving seat, dragging off her precious, and she knows next to nothing about me. Only the fact that I pitch up in Bill's A8 gives me any licence to take the girls out. Even so, Yvonne's mother looks at me through slit eyes when I arrive.

'All right darling, I'm at the hairdressers tonight, so I won't see you until dinner. Pella's staying on to make you something, okay?'

'All right, mam.' A little impatiently, I think. Yvonne's mother should hear the language the girls use when they are out of parental earshot.

Kirsty is slightly shorter and dumpier than the other two, even if her house is even bigger than Yvonne's. Her slight shortfall in the currency of looks makes her marginally subordinate in the eyes of the other two. There's an unexpected hierarchy, just like there is with the boys, only more subtle. I empathise with Kirsty and her lower standing, but she does have a trump card to play: Kirsty has horses and the girls all ride. Currency comes in many forms.

I get all this from the short time I spend driving them to and from school, to each other's houses and the couple of times I've driven them up to Glasgow for 'proper' shopping.

They talk a lot. Sometimes they tease me and I pretend to be teased. It's all attention. Yvonne has a tendency towards flirtation, which I fear might get her into trouble in the wrong circumstances. They're all socially assured in a way that I can never remember being. I can mix it now that I'm a big grown-up, but self-assurance is never the thing I'm feeling.

I try and keep the ride smooth when I'm driving them to school. After I have dropped them off, and they have walked through the school gates without looking back, I am free for a while. One of my few perks is that I have free rein with the Audi if Bill doesn't need it. He even pays for the petrol or, at least, he puts it on his petrol account.

I've covered a few miles this way. Even though the Motherwell district is far from being my home, I do at worst reside here. Like Bill, with his mental template of the big plan, I like to have a good sense of the layout of where I am. Something of this goes back to my time on despatch. I wouldn't have said that it was the equivalent of having done the 'Knowledge', but I did have a better than working knowledge of London. I need that sense here too, so I've been up to Paisley and Greenock and round to Largs, I've been around most major roads in Lanarkshire. I go south, but never as far as the English border. I've been to Edinburgh, but no further. I set my northern limit at Stenhousemuir. In any case, having the car for too long is taking the piss out of Bill's generosity.

When I'm tired I get a boost from the big V8 up front. It's the sort of feeling of being connected to the power that I used to have when I was on the bike. The engine's smooth and refined most of the time, but there's an off-beat growl that you can really feel through certain ranges of acceleration.

I'm tired most of the time now, though it's not uncommon to find myself occasionally shot through with a kind of nervous energy. I'm better when I'm actually doing stuff: I think the tiredness comes from eating at myself when I'm not occupied.

Today I cross the Antonine wall and take a country route to Denny before swinging back down the A80 and skirting Glasgow on the M73. Motorways are similar wherever they are; I remain the same in all environments: a small dot on the periphery.

Bill is having doubts about our project. I detect that. There's a big difference between having a sound idea and being faced with problematic realities. Bill's divided between a set of risks which may be impossible to overcome and the fact that this is probably his only shot at saving the house and his standard of family life. He can't accept something like that. He can only go forward. There's no question of going back or contemplating reduced circumstances. He never gets tired. I seem to be the only one who's like that. I change down a gear and accelerate, just for the rush.

Before long I've been out for hours, so I pull into some services for something to eat, just like I used to do when I worked The Route and was out for three days at a stretch. Even that is forever ago on the odd occasions that it pops into my mind. I don't like to think – it's enervating. I eat my bruschetta and sip my overpriced coffee and try and picture Lauren the first time I collected her from school.

It was a new duty for me. Justine had been unexpectedly kept at the optician's and Bill was somewhere unreachable. The school was a bugger to find. When I arrived, Lauren was sitting on a bench a short way from the gates. I was supposed to be picking her up, but I didn't want to get out of the car quite yet. She hadn't noticed me, parked just across the road.

She put her bag down and sighed visibly. This was the first time I'd seen her outside of her usual, voluble self and her face seemed different. Without the mobility of speech she looked sad, thoughtful maybe in a way that reminded me of... I'd imagined that all teenagers just got straight onto the phone as soon as they had a quiet moment. Modern kids can't stand the quiet, which is why they have to giggle or squeak or pretend to fart in the brief fermata before the film starts at the cinema, puncturing the mood and any possibility of escaping into fantasy.

She looks at her watch in an idle way and then at her feet, which she shuffles into place. She, unaware of me, and I of anything but the thoughts in my head and the fine lines on the skin of my hands still holding the wheel. I project myself onto my teenage self, falling short in the attempt. I breathe as lightly as I can to keep corporeal things from entering my state of mind, drawing my focus down to a tight beam, away from the lines on my hands to the form of a young girl on a quiet bench who has had to wait alone. My sense of touch falls away until there is only thought and no sensation of mass or texture or the aches of my old injuries. Time spins out the seconds and I breathe only to stop myself from sliding into oblivion. Then, as if she can feel the infinitesimal weight of my gaze on the wave of her hair she raises her head, sees me and smiles...

I've dallied too long in the services and will be late collecting them if I don't get a move on. I've used up the school day just driving around. In the services I felt almost normal for a second, then it went. I hammer down the road.

EUAN

Sometime after sunset Euan picks me up in his Evo and takes me over to his place. We pass the new, big houses and the golf course and head in towards suburbia. Here the houses are almost as new, but a fraction of the size. Euan's is a medium-sized detached place on a typical estate, space for two cars on the front, minimal garden, detached in name more than fact: there's only room for one layer of air molecules between his and next door's.

He backs onto the drive carefully next to Debbie's two-door Suzuki. I have met her briefly once when she and Euan were passing through the Waverley. She's small and pretty in a footballers' wives kind of way. Her appearance has been managed to such a degree that she is supra human, perfect, made from non-deformable materials, beyond normal considerations such as perspiration. She and Euan aren't married, though I'm sure Debbie *thinks* they are.

The house too might have been airbrushed into existence. Everything is modern and clean and angular. There is no dirt and there never has been.

I stand in the living room whilst Euan checks his messages on the computer upstairs. Debbie comes through from the kitchen with a glass of lemonade. I hadn't realised I was thirsty until I saw the drink, but now realise I am. The outside of the glass is picked out in a rather over-ornate pattern that I guess to be her taste.

'Thanks.' I say.

Some seconds pass without further words. Although she hasn't been staring, I am aware that she has weighed me up. I am a scruffy presence in her pristine home.

She doesn't have a facial expression. Perhaps that's the secret of her prettiness: she could be a picture. I wonder what her original hair colour was, whether it's one amongst the many highlights or darker strands. I'm estimating her beautification bill. I bet this whole set-up is her idea – she can put up with Euan as long as she gets a decent place and all the rest. I know she only has a part-time job somewhere that would never cover the expenses. Then I see something beyond the lack of expression, a kind of steeliness in the eye. Possibly she's the boss in this relationship. Euan's a hard man and hard men are often easily emotionally manipulated.

'Sit down,' she says, 'he's going to be a long time if he's doing emails.'

So I sit, and now I have to have a conversation with a woman on my own. Time was this wouldn't have been a problem, but time has marginalised me to the point that I no longer have common ground with anyone. I sip at my lemonade slowly to cover up the palpable gaps in communication. I'm leaning back onto the settee in my knackered leather jacket; she's settled into an armchair opposite, but sitting upright.

‘You’re going out with some shoes?’

‘Sorry, are we?’ I haven’t been told what I’m doing here. I rarely know what I’m going to be doing. Apparently, one has to be ready to do anything.

‘Yes, good, they’re filling up the spare room.’

‘Right, well, we’ll be on it soon.’

‘He’ll be ages yet if he has to reply to anything. His typing’s terrible. I tell him I’ll type for him if he tells me what he wants to say. I can do forty words a minute.’

‘Can you? That’s fast.’ Even sipping I’ve reached the end of my lemonade too quickly. The last bit makes an uncouth slurping sound as it drains into my mouth. Then I have to hold an empty glass. I wish Euan could do forty words a minute, then we could get on with business. Debbie has one of those neat figures and I can’t stop myself trying to picture it, which is making me feel uncomfortable and widening the gap between seconds. She could be eighteen or twenty-eight, no kids yet. I bet Euan is infertile. That would be just right.

‘You’re not Scottish are you, John, where do you come from?’

‘No, I’m not really sure, London.’

‘You don’t know where you come from?’

‘No, yes, not exactly.’ *Turn it round.* ‘What about you? Motherwell?’

‘Wishaw.’

‘Not too far to come, then?’

‘Not really, it’s a bit different.’

‘Where did you meet, if you don’t mind me asking?’

'At the gym.'

I suppose they would.

She goes on. 'I work there. Euan knows Charlie, the owner. Charlie offered him a partnership in a new gym in Hamilton and he turned it down. It's really successful now. Euan's been kicking himself ever since. He never goes over to Hamilton if he can help it.'

'That's tough. It's difficult to make the right decision sometimes.'

'No.'

Something in the tone tells me it hasn't been Euan doing the kicking. She didn't need to tell me this, but she wants me to know. Possible she tells anyone who will listen. It's not an issue that's going to go away any time soon.

There's another one of those awkward pauses, filled with me picturing Debbie working out at the gym. My glass is a dead weight now that it's empty and there's no table on which to set it down. In such surroundings it can't be placed on the carpet, but it has at least given me an idea.

'Mind if I use your bathroom?'

'Why, are you going to have a bath?'

I'm not too sure of the pitch of her humour. She hasn't smiled. 'No, I…'

'Straight ahead up the stairs.'

What was I going to say, "No, I want to take a piss/slash/have a tinkle?" She gets up at the same as me and takes my glass, which means that our fingers brush slightly. I feel the first small pulse of a nascent erection.

The bathroom is one of those modernist, minimalist masterpieces. There's a set of his-and-hers sinks set into black slate. I am very, very careful not to miss the toilet pan. I wash my hands in cold water to distract me from other thoughts.

Euan is in a back room typing with one finger. I know what he's writing because he's mouthing out the words. I don't bother him. I glance into the master bedroom with its bed wreathed in brown covers. I picture Euan rising from it in the mornings. I bet he wears shorts, even down to breakfast, first thing the long, leisurely piss. He's not the sort to wake during the night, so his bladder will be bursting full of lager from the night before. Never a hangover, quickly and easily over the beard with his electric shaver, looking approvingly at himself in the mirror. Debbie will be downstairs already, making breakfast. He'll feel his chin for perfection before tidying up the rough spots and moving into the shower. Too much shampoo, too much shower gel, insufficiently rinsed, spending more time than necessary on his cock, back into the bedroom, naked with the curtains open, dabbing with the towel, talc, deodorant, that unspeakable aftershave, a touch of hair gel to catch that unkempt style just right, a last look in the bathroom mirror, setting out a new set of clothes for the new day and down to breakfast.

Debbie's washing my glass in the kitchen when I get back downstairs, limiting its potential for contaminating the premises. At least it saves me from more conversation and revelation. Instead, I stand and stare out of the front window, at the other houses with their multiple occupancy. Everyone has someone. Except me.

We load the boxes of trainers into the boot of the Evo. We soon run out of space and carry on to the back seat. Euan pulls one out and says, 'Look at that, perfect.' Like most trainers it seems over-sized and over-elaborate. They are fakes. He wants me to concur that they are indistinguishable from the real thing, but why the fuck should I know anything about the real thing?

The street girls are out already as we work our way across town, shivering in their miniskirts, arms folded against the cold. Other young women are out, looking much the same. I'd forgotten it was a Friday. This makes more sense of Euan's comment about missing a night's work to drop off these knock-offs. He has lots more too, in a friend's garage. I look at the women and feel cold on their behalf, even sitting in a warm car with my coat on.

There hasn't been any mention of pay. Seems that, if you're part of a team, then there are responsibilities. I wasn't at the meeting where the roster of duties and responsibilities was tabled up. Theoretically, I suppose, if I had my own agenda, then I might be able to call on some back-up from one or other of the boys, but how likely is that? All my business is Bill's business. Perhaps I'll get a drink out of it.

The drive is quite long and complicated. Euan's not

too good on routes, but he was born here, so he recognises where he is. It's clear why there won't be time for any door work tonight after all this.

The geezer we're going to see is just someone who spoke to someone who spoke to Euan when he was working on one of his door shifts. We're not even meeting him at a premises, just some car park next to a recreation area. Delivering in this way is well within my experience, so I'm not expecting much, but when we arrive there's even less. Our contact hasn't arrived, even though we are late. We sit in the car waiting and waiting. Euan doesn't seem bothered, then he's a bit bothered, then he's really quite bothered. He doesn't say much, simply gives the impression of someone chain smoking in the absence of cigarettes. I've been watching the time and it hasn't even been twenty minutes yet. I've had to wait much longer than that on jobs like these.

Euan doesn't like it at all. I've observed that he's a bit of a tight arse when it comes to money. He'll buy a round all right, but he won't go until last to reduce his chance of having to come round again. I bet that's why he wouldn't front up for the gym partnership. Right now he can see a deal disappearing and all the profits with it. He's holding tight onto the steering wheel.

'Fuck,' he says, 'I've got his number.'

He pulls out his mobile and searches through the numbers. His lips move as he works through the menus. I only get our half of the conversation.

'No… what you say?…You say what?… You say

what?... No. I don't think so... No... You don't know me... You don't know me.... You don't know me... You're not getting this, you don't know me... No. You won't... You won't. No. You don't know me. YOU DON'T KNOW ME'

There's a pause while he identifies that the other party has hung up. Euan trains too much. It gives him a slightly drawn and on-the-edge look. I am stuck in the car with him.

'Problem?' I'm expecting an outburst, but he seems to be getting control of himself.

'He's not coming, says he's been to someone else.'

'Fucker.'

'Aye.'

'We doing anything?'

'No.'

He thinks for a moment, 'No, later.'

I don't get my drink. I don't even go back to Euan's house to help him unload. He just takes me straight back to my dark garage where I spend five minutes pondering what I might have for dinner before giving up and eating a bottle of wine.

THE ROUTE

The old route collapsed so suddenly and with such violence that I still have nightmares. There are images which are now burned permanently into my retinas, as if I have stared too long into a horror-shaped light bulb. Trying to blank that stuff out requires an assortment of strategies mostly based on keeping oneself occupied – not so easy without an occupation. One day I had a job, a nice apartment, a works van, a sports bike and bundles of cash. The next day only the cash remained.

I understood that I had to leave, and quickly, but I had no plan. I'd already made preparations for leaving before I'd even left for my last three days of delivering on The Route, but not for anything beyond the act of leaving. So I just caught any bus that was heading out of London, with a few clothes crowded out by the wads of cash in my holdall.

I spent time in hotels trying to stay ahead of the images in my mind. I couldn't be sure whether anyone was actually after me, but that wasn't what mattered most, purely the act of putting time and distance between me and the source of my trouble. I occupied a living nightmare where all normal standards of human behaviour had been suborned by the forces of acquisition.

The best sort of establishments would have suited me best, but they are insufficiently anonymous. You have to swipe a credit card when you check in, and I don't have a credit card. I have lived for years in a cash economy and I don't have a proper identity or background to make me credit-worthy. So, I had to stick to middling and lower-class places where they don't ask too many questions, one day a Travelodge, the next a suburban B & B. Weeks elapsed as I passed from place to place. Sometimes I wouldn't even check out, simply leave the right money in the room and hope that it would find its way to reception rather than to the housekeeping staff. Time has no steady component in this sort of situation: half an hour waiting for a bus can become an eternity; half a day can slip away sitting in a library. It was December and the weather too inclement for spending time outside. At Christmas I hid in a room with packs of sandwiches and a couple of bottles of wine, no cards or carols, no friends or relatives, no season of joy. Even with the telly on I could hear the sounds of jollity in other parts of the hotel. Two bottles of strong red will make you sleep, but not without waking up dehydrated many times through the night with your head pounding.

December became January became February. It was clear that my money wasn't going to last as long as I'd thought. I'd never counted it, merely pushed most of what I was paid for working The Route into the bottom drawer of a kitchen unit in my apartment. I hadn't even counted when Dave was handing it over on my irregular, if lucrative, paydays. It was simply lots more money than I was getting through and the surplus was there if I needed it. I needed it, but the physical quantity was definitely diminishing faster than I'd thought possible.

Despite my criminal past, I come without connections. Paid employees don't get connected. I've hung around the underworld with monsters without ever being asked to join the monster club. There is no system of support: the money is the support. Hence, I don't have the wherewithal to go about getting a false passport or a pukka replacement identity or proper set-up. I am a non-person who survives by having the cash to get what I need. The cash was going too quickly, so I was forced to move further downmarket.

The dreams of others can be a nightmare for you. Some B & Bs exist solely to service families on benefit. There are permanent residents here, trapped in a parallel world of homeless benefit reliance, perched precariously over a roofless drop on one side and a stiff climb to so-called respectability on the other, one or two parents with three kids occupying two rooms only. These are people with *THE WRONG STUFF* written in invisible letters on their CVs – visible to everyone but themselves, that is. They just don't have the ropes and tackle to make that climb. It's more likely they'll fall in the attempt.

That's where I found myself next, waiting out the winter and watching over my money, soulless and unconnected, the bulge in my bag acting like a beacon to those around me. Red, I think, is the colour of money. In these places, sums of money above a scatter of cash are the stuff of dreams.

More indiscriminate time, until I was tired of the cries of children and the shouts of desperate parents trying to get a moment's peace. There are few places without children, but a chance encounter with a short-termer in a common area told me where I might find one.

I arrive in Birmingham on a weekday, like a tramp. I have two pairs of trousers: some jeans which I hate, but lose me better in a crowd, and a good pair of grey wool trousers which have become shiny and matted like the weathered moleskins of a coachman. The only footwear I have is a pair of decent Derby boots which have remained unpolished for months and are showing it. If my dark blue, pin-striped blazer hadn't become so screwed up in my holdall I might pass for tarnished respectable, but it's too far gone for that. So too my leather jacket, which I wear all the time. It cost twelve hundred pounds originally, when the money was coming in. It needs feeding badly and is cracked from being in the rain too much. Still, I have to keep a close eye on it: leather jackets like this are as good as currency in the circles in which I travel. I had an excellent wool overcoat and that got stolen from a pub during the three minutes I was off having a piss one night in January. Twelve hundred pounds has to last me months now, to include accommodation, all food and travel. I am obviating the travel by settling down in one place for a while.

My leather jacket is not so good now, but quality will still out. My own qualities are all out and found wanting. I have good taste. That is all the good that can be said of me. I put it down to good breeding. I will never now procreate, so my branch of the line dies out with me. It will be a good thing, because I was never able to avoid some atavistic tendencies that have led me to abandon all that was worthwhile in myself and stoop to low practices.

In the absence of my wool coat, over my leather jacket I have taken to wearing a cheaply bought US combat jacket, type M65. It once belonged to someone called Pte. Enright. His name survives inside in indelible marker. I picture him in an artillery bunker on a sandy escarpment in Vietnam, sitting in a dug-outconstructed from sand bags, olive steel corrugated revetment material and those plates formed with lines of circular holes. Stencilled green boxes are piled around, many empty: creamed beef; processed cheese; boiled potatoes; tinned water; toilet tissue; 303 rounds (ball). He's sitting out of the sun between fire missions, beneath thick netting, wondering whether he should be cleaning out his jam-prone firearm once again even though he hasn't had to use it this entire posting. He passes another Camel to his buddy, who hands back his Zippo in turn. Engraved upon it, it says: *Though I walk through the Valley of Death, I fear no evil, for I am the evilest Mother fucker in the Valley.* Two men sleeping in a corner are rangers from Special Ops who appeared in the early morning looking for a place to crash, half way home from some unspeakable objective they have completed in a supposedly gook-sympathetic village a dozen hard clicks away through 'rat' infested country. They had a hungry look when they came in, like vampires who have fed on blood and fed again, but are doomed to relentless appetite. Enright wonders whether they have trophies amongst their kit. He's heard of this kind of thing. Even if they dry those trophies in the sun, the humidity will rot them away like everything else, and he scratches at his sweat rash once again and draws on his Camel. The packet shows a dry desert and pyramids. The old man fought in Africa before crossing over to Sicily with the pretty girls and the wine; Enright sits in the steaming jungle waiting for orders with music fading in and out on the forces radio, '*We gotta get outta this place...*'

Enright's combat jacket is piss-poor in the rain, but it at least keeps the worst of it getting through to my leather one underneath. Combat jackets were what the alternative types wore when I was a kid. It took me right back when I found one in an army surplus store between destinations, right back to 1975, wondering how I'm going to manage to grow into my expectations. I'm not, it turns out. 1975. Enright would have been back by then, one way or another. When you're buying a garment like this, with a history, you have to select for size and condition, whether there are rips and tears and holes and repairs. Some of this ex-combat stuff has stains and ruptures that bring forth images of blood spattering onto lush undergrowth and blast-blackened ground. Enright's looks whole, but on the whole I don't reckon he made it back intact, maybe to community indifference or boxed and draped under a flag. 'Each man thinks poorly of himself for never having been a soldier,' said Mr Johnson. Others think poorly of themselves for selling their immortal souls for money and denigrating their family names.

I arrive in Birmingham by coach. The journey has been broken up by enjoying the regular passage of the stewardess's behind at eye level. It's all gone according to schedule right up until a delay for getting into our designated slot at the bus station. I miss the bike or even the van, but not its contents. I see myself reflected in a newsagent's window looking like a down-and-out seeking a pitch and the next bottle of Diamond White. Perhaps it's not far from the truth.

I have already lost count of the places I've lain my head. Whatever happens I will stick in this new place for a while just to catch up with myself. My contact has told me there are no kids allowed and no one bothers anyone else, which is what I need. I have sparse few directions, and Birmingham is an unfamiliar place, but I find my new home quite quickly, after a few enquiries and one or two claims of ignorance.

At what passes for check-in I find that they're not really set up for cash, but someone senior smells the readies and sorts it out. I find out later that no one actually pays directly. The place was once a grand station hotel built into the corner of a new development, but the glass in the main entrance has now been whitewashed and only one of the four doors is in use. There's a small desk inside the foyer with a TV on it, and a guy who's seen everything twice to watch who's going in and out. That's about it. The rooms have all been subdivided into half rooms with a bed and an easy chair and a fridge that chatters through the night. The fridge is there to keep the drink cool, because the place is full of ex-cons and alcoholics. No one works. Everyone is paid benefit, which goes straight to the owners of the 'hotel' to pay for the room. The 'guests' then get their pocket money to spend on drink and whatever food they can be bothered to procure from the local takeaways in between the effects of alcoholic malnourishment. The off licence, barely three hundred yards up the road, does sterling business in the most cost-effective ways of getting off your head.

Through the night I am kept awake by hacking coughs from froth-corrupted lungs. The reek of cigarette smoke somehow bleeds through the walls. My few clothes are stale with it. Some guests make madhouse noises in their distant rooms. I don't know how many rooms there are, maybe more than a hundred now that all the lounge and restaurant spaces have been divided up for occupation. The drains must bubble with spent yeast and thick urine from hard, shrivelled livers. I have never seen one woman. I'm not sure they're even allowed through the door. When I see my fellow guests they look like the dry middle-aged men of my childhood with their sandpaper faces and oiled dandruffy hair who used wait with myself and my mother in the barber's shop, me wondering what styptic pencils were for and whether they were anything to do with solving the crossword puzzles that kept my father so uncommunicative in the early evenings when we were allowed to watch the TV, as long as the sound was turned off.

Some men never go out, so they must send others to the offy to get their stuff in. Others live in the pub until closing time. The limited number of bathrooms are foul from overuse, even though they are cleaned every other day. Some rooms must still be en suite, but certainly not mine. At night I stay in my dug-out listening for the enemy and ignoring any knocks on my door. I guess the door knockers wander around hoping to get lucky for 'friendship' or free alcohol or to push themselves into you in any way they can. I am living in a William Burroughs story and all I think about is sex. Around the corner, beneath the railway arches, is a massage parlour with a red plastic awning above its door, brightly lit against the black Victorian brickwork. Sometimes I see one or other of the girls coming out to buy soft drinks from the shop, neatly plucked eyebrows, skin-tight tops, bare necks and décolletages. How many of the guests here have enough cash left over to go in for 'extras'? Maybe you can get credit for that kind of thing, with unfavourable rates. The girls, for all their professional obligations, seem somehow pure and unruffled next to the occupants of the hotel. I can't make judgements about them anyway, not from my vantage point. For the same reason I could never countenance using their services: going into an establishment like that would be like entering my old world with all its consequences.

Instead I go to watch a film, sometimes two a day, or hide in the big bookshop with its easy chairs. My bag goes with me, except when I go into the museum and art gallery where bags aren't allowed for security reasons. I have a method of secreting large amounts in my combat jacket. Much of what is left now is in fifties – I've deliberately used up the smaller denominations – and quite large amounts can take up relatively little space. I'm never bagless on cleaning days however, once a week when they change the sheets, and so the museum has to remain out of bounds at those times.

How the other guests would love to get hold of my money. Any one of them is a threat. They could blow it all in a day at the bookies – get drunk first to settle any last ghosts of inhibition and then just bet on everything going. At night I can feel their avarice and part of my attention always rests on my cash. Every time I see someone else I know that they know about my stash and are working on ways to get at it. One of them will attract your attention while the other makes a grab and runs off with it. They'll divide it up later, only they won't when the grabber sees just how much there is and blows off the distracter. There was only a shit black and white TV in the room anyway, so I'll get away now and fuck the lot of them, only after I've just stepped into this pub.

You can get through days walking about, reading books, having something to eat, looking at the headstones in the broken-down graveyard, falling asleep in the cinema, trying to find a city-centre pub that isn't full of tossers and people watching big-screen TV. But you get tired of the smoke when you get back to your room, number 229, thinking about people you've left behind and can never see again, simply by dint of wondering why you no longer think about them.

I never left the city for the entire few months of my stay. In the day the drunks staggered up and down the streets and sometimes fell down along with their prized four packs of beer in plastic webbing. That was enough. I'd figured that I'd needed to settle for that while, but I now needed to settle somewhere else, somewhere that was my own place where I could stay unmolested and anonymous, while I still had enough money to pay a deposit and plenty of rent in advance. If I didn't, then the sea of questionable humanity at the hotel would dye me in its own colours. I'd turn grey and, with skin like sandpaper, walk into the barber's asking for products (Macassar oil, menthol cream, rubber ferrules – all sizes). Beyond that would come a gradual ossification – a true setting of the bones – until movement was no longer possible.

The library wouldn't let me use the internet without a

card, so I had to spend money in internet cafes finding somewhere to live. It needed to be cheap and available for cash without references, which turned out to be far from easy. What you can do sometimes, however, is see pictures of a place on a website, so you know what you're dealing with. In the follow-up phone calls I used my best voice without sounding too posh. Neutral and businesslike, 'No, I've just sold a place and I haven't rented for years.'; 'No, I was working overseas...Guyana on an international development project...no, years...no, I have some relocation funds from the company...yes, Thursday. Look forward to seeing you then.'

Which is how I found a little place on an ex-municipal estate in the East Midlands with cash up front and a year's tenancy guaranteed, as well as a new name and hair style.

DEEP

I hadn't really thought that being part of a criminal gang involved sitting around bars and darkened rooms talking shit and playing cards, but sometimes it's just like that. We've all convened at the works for the evening while we wait for Bill and news from some endeavour. He is seeing someone about the inside angle. It's all very hopeful and will move us on immeasurably. Even so, I wonder whether this would all be better done by phone or email. It's the twenty-first century. Mal smells of stale fags and body odour and it would be better to be in a different county.

To pass the time we've been playing Texas Hold-'em poker for maybe a couple of hours in the old secretaries' room. There were two secretaries in the old days, long laid off. Now dust settles slowly on the desks and cabinets. Only Bill's office gets a clean, by Justine every once in a while. Below us the warehouse is sad and empty, yearning for the dynamics of business. It's a forlorn place sometimes, like the very limits of the solar system, right out where the sun's warmth fails to make an impact. I'm trapped here, far from the Earth and all its glories.

Euan and Deep have played cards before. A lot. I give

myself away too easily: it's in my expression. Mal doesn't have sufficient attention span to plan out his moves, but he has brought loads of cash that he doesn't seem to mind losing. I'm keen to wind down and bow out before I'm through my meagre resources, but I'm thinking that the boys won't like that too much. There are systems of etiquette in place. I pick up on them okay, even if I don't like them. No one is sympathetic or accommodating as they might be in more gentile society, it's all to do with showing no weakness, fronting yourself up all the time, making like you give no quarter. Even so, there is an honesty about it, or more a predictability perhaps. As individuals they make themselves count by posturing, bluff and noise. They play cards in the same way. I would prefer pontoon, in opposition to a banker, where you only have to play the odds, and not against goons who base their self-worth on superficial notions of who looks best at any given time.

I'm probably being unfair to Deep. I think in other circumstances he'd be a stand-up citizen. He talks about family a lot and he has a really genuine appreciation of his parents and older sister. His parents are second generation with residual cultural values from the old country. Deep is as Scottish as you come and now he's found a place just beneath the respectable radar where he can graft his way wherever it takes. He has a pocket full of drugs even now, though I've never seen him take any. He just sells, sometimes moves goods around. Every bloke I know here is into some scam or traffic or way of making extra. It's natural for them. They lock into a pre-existing undercurrent, one that has caught me up and dragged me down.

Mal is looking drunk. We have already worked through a bottle of Bell's. Euan is licking his lips as he gathers in the pot once again. Deep's narrowing his eyes, thinking of getting even.

Euan says something like 'stellya keg'. The more the boys drink, the more they slip into dialect, of which a proportion is impenetrable to a nancy southerner like myself. I guess he's saying something like 'Read 'em and weep'. He and Deep have also been drinking some alco-pop rubbish that has probably been semi-officially appropriated from one of the clubs at which they work. I'll stick with the whisky: I'm disinclined to drink anything that's blue in colour.

Deep rubs the last remains of the bruise he got from his run-in with Atil. It's healed quickly. He's young. I'm not sure when I got to the point where people in their twenties seem young. I have put on too much mileage in every way possible. I slug back my drink and resolve to win something back before the night's out. Then Bill arrives.

He doesn't look too happy.

'Drink?' I offer him the bottle and he pours out a treble.

We stop playing and put down our cards. Mal puts his down face up, which will void the hand. I know I would have won too.

'It's a no go,' says Bill.

Euan looks up at him, 'Why?'

'He wouldn't go for it without a lot more cash.'

'Fucking cunt. We'll go and see him.'

'No, it's too much attention.'

From what I've divined Euan has set this up. It's someone connected with the security company who are contracted to the exhibition hall. We could have had inside information and maybe even inside management on the night we go in. What could have become a certainty remains a variable. It's also a human variable, which are the worst kind. When we've talked about the heist it's been dealing with the security personnel that has been the most vexed question. Of course, there has been a lot of bravado, but I'm sure that even the most gung-ho of us has realised that we are all fucked if the security team can get us bottled up or get the Police down on us before we can do what we have to do. We can spy on security guards from the outside all we like, we can get inside when they're not there and look at their set-up when they're not there, but we can't know what strategies they have in place in the event of a break-in without insider knowledge.

'What did he want?'

'Eighty grand.'

'Fuck what?'

'Said it would pay off his mortgage.'

We're in this for the money. We're in it because we need the money. We can't come up with eighty grand. I could just about round up eighty quid.

'He wouldn't shift. He wanted it up front with no guarantees that he'd have the information. I bought all the drinks – there was nothing more I could do.'

Bill looks more tired than I've ever seen him before. It's late at night. I didn't get up early, but I know Bill did. Justine's car had to go for a service and Bill took her to work and Lauren to school.

Euan's ready with something else he wants to say, but Bill's expression says 'don't'. He takes the whisky bottle and heads out of the room. He's going to sit in his office and think. I never like to see a man take a blow, something of it hits me too.

The mood changes in the room. Where there was a touch of light-heartedness, now the hang-dogs of excess alcohol and belligerence show their faces. I have to drink the blue stuff, which is a chemical broth with no redeeming features other than its alcoholic content. It would be best ice cold rather than tepid. It tastes like blue dye.

We play some more, in relative quiet. I want to go home. Deep pulls out a knife and starts cleaning his nails.

'What the fuck's that?' says Mal.

'What's what?'

'That wee thingy. You call that a knife?' He's attempting an Australian accent, I think. 'Now this is a knife.' He reaches round to the back of his trousers and brings out what looks like the modern equivalent of a bayonet. 'You can make someone think with something like that.' He plonks it on the desk with a thud.

Deep looks unimpressed, 'See you with your mild steel. This is your state-of-the-art US special forces, Teflon coated, no drag in or out.'

'It's tiny, man'

Deep's taking on board just how drunk Mal is. He settles for a hard look rather than a vocal response.

So far Euan hasn't looked up from his cards. 'Now, then boys, this is a blade.' Apparently it was down a sock or in a sheath attached to his leg. It's one of those metal butterfly knifes with a split handle that closes around the blade and flicks around to make it ready. He clacks it into operation with a flourish. He's obviously practiced. Anyway, it's enough of a show to make them all laugh out loud for a whole minute before they all fall silent at the same instant and look at me.

'All right, John,' says Euan, 'we've shown you ours – let's have a look at yours.'

'Mine's at home.'

I know that they don't shoot you much around here. You can get shot, walking home from the pub, by someone on the pillion of a motorcycle. It's a new sort of tradition, but it's not the general way of things. If someone takes exception to you then they'll tend to take that exception to you at close quarters. They come at you with a knife, so, you're in the street and some fucker comes up and cuts you on your hand or face to make a point, or he may want to really stripe you so that you know he's been. Maybe it will stop there or maybe he'll use the blade as an extension of his fist and punch it into you a few times. You might survive that, but you might perish from a small scratch that catches your femoral artery. It's all a bit of a lottery, so the condemned might live while someone who was just being given a lesson bleeds his whole life out on a street corner.

You learn all this stuff from your colleagues. They love talking about it, the bouncers in particular. They're all fucking gladiators. They bring it all out for effect when there are quiet moments or when they're trying to big themselves up. It's schoolyard stuff, but it gets you wondering what might lead you to want to vent someone's crimson on a quiet evening over some minor transgression. How would you land on that as a proportional response? *Best if I cleave into this guy's bodily tissue and kick him over while he's waiting to catch up with what's happened.*

'What's that, John? You have'nae got a blade. Why not? They've all got them. It's nae right because they won't think twice if you cannae defend yourself.'

'I'm just a driver.'

'Just a driver, fuck. You're not always in your car, are you? What about when you're in town?'

'Sometimes I just don't bring it out.'

'And what if you meet someone who's after your hide?'

'For instance?'

Euan's not quite *au fait* with this type of reasoning.

'How'd you know who you're gonnae meet? What about one of Osman's boys? They're all cunts.'

'What would they want with me?'

'They don't need to want anything. They're just head cases. They'll open you up just to see what colour you are inside. I'll tell you about Osman. He's the worst head fuck there is. You dinnae know what you're dealing with. Deep, you remember. They had that Kosovan girl, right? One of those illegal immigrants.'

'Right, they had them sucking old men's cocks for thirty pound a head [Euan laughs], up at a nice semi in Hamilton. Anyway, she gets homesick for her mammy or something and decides to run off one day and make a phone call. What was her name, Maggie?'

'Aye, call her Maggie. They don't use their real names because no one knows how to say them. And she's just seventeen.'

'Fifteen, I heard, Euan, just off the boat. Anyway, she can't fucking speak English well enough to know how to use the phone and it's one of those wi' only card slots, so she's got nae chance. So they catch up with her real easy. Next thing is, she's up in front of Osman and he's no too happy about it, so you know what he does?'

He goes quiet for a moment waiting for me to say 'no'.

'What does he do?' I say.

'He gets the girl, little Maggie and they take her to one of his fast food places, a chip shop, after hours. They put a squash ball in her mouth and tape it up so she can't shout out and they get all her clothes off and push her arm deep down into the hot fat and hold her there and hold her with the fat spitting up into her face and her screaming against the ball and keep her there until the arm's cooked. Right?'

We're all quiet in the room. I get the point – there are bad people out there and the only way to deal with them is to be a mean motherfucker yourself. Which is fine because, if we all go around stabbing each other, then only the decent people will be left.

Bill comes back in. He brings a palpable sense of resignation. I guess he feels that the security situation, along with the other problems, may be too much to overcome. The whisky bottle is empty. Perhaps we'll toss a coin to see who's driving home before I end up doing it anyway. What am I doing to myself? In my life I have already seen horrible things. I didn't ask to and now they've taken something of me away. Nothing is planned. I just drifted onto the wrong side one day and found that I couldn't get back. Light, truth and beauty slid away leaving darkness, lies and cruelty. There are new standards here. I'm too tired to argue and I can't lose too much face with the boys. The next time I have use of the car I head off to a hardware store to get a knife. I know I should be down at the army surplus inquiring about what they might have under the counter, but that's not me, so I find an outdoor market and spend time looking at cheap copies of wood-handled Opinel knives in all the sizes from little finger to forearm.

Stupid as it is, I deliberate long and hard about what length might be considered okay by the boys without it being too unwieldy to fit in my pocket. I also need it to be innocuous enough to be explained away to the Police if I'm stopped, 'Sorry officer, I was just taking some cuttings in the garden and had to pop out for some rooting powder, My wee wife will be wondering where I am.'

When I have decided and got it home, I age it with some selective scratching and judicious application of soil from the garden. I don't want it looking like I've just bought it. My untruths are subtle and well-planned; my life a whole lot less so.

STEEL

There are things to do. Bill seems to like it. There are few changes in his demeanour most of the time. He's not dour, just undemonstrative. I look for subtle signs. The weather stays within narrow bounds: it's grey; it drizzles; a wind comes up more or less. Instead of big changes, you notice small alterations within the range. It's the same with Bill.

We're up early. I drive Bill up to the works and we collect the van. I never know quite what we're doing most of the time. Today it seems we're delivering just a few boxes of condoms. He doesn't need me for that and we don't need the van, unless it's for keeping up the professional image: an employee and the apparatus of delivery. Perhaps it's bad form to show up in a flash car – seems like you're making too much money out of the customer.

It's pitiful how low stock levels have got. When I used to visit Bill during the time of The Route, the shelves were stacked full of boxes of condoms, lubricants, sex-aids and sundries. There were staff too, a whole empire from Bill down to the part-time cleaner. Now it's the ruins of an empire, bare bone archaeological traces, the footings in the ground with none of the walls.

The three boxes we load into the van look lost and forlorn on the load floor. We drive off, westwards through East Kilbride. It takes ages, of course. It's a huge urban sprawl of interconnected towns. Perhaps it just looks like that to an outsider.

Empty vans make much more noise than full ones. The floor shimmies and the side panels crash over the bumps. The three lonely boxes slide about on the corners.

Bill's prophylactic business covers a big area. It started off with a few pubs, supplying vending machines for the gents. Bill spent his small redundancy package from the steel industry setting up the business at home. The vending machines were converted from old chewing gum machines: *Beech Nut* and *Juicy Fruit*, stripped down, rejigged and repainted in Bill's corporate green. The revolution came, he said, when he persuaded landlords to accept machines in the ladies as well, doubling product exposure and, surprisingly, more than doubling yield.

I can see Bill traipsing around every pub in the district, further and further afield, always personal contact, sometimes getting knocked back, sometimes scoring, getting himself established, building gradually through force of personality and dogged persistence, making the connections to move into wholesale, expanding the product range, trying to find new markets, getting into business with my old boss Terence as a distributor for our stuff, adding big profits onto a the back of a firm business basis, getting a better car, moving into a new house, feeling like you've done it all off your own bat.

I follow Bill's instructions and drive through the morning traffic, left, right, straight on, third exit, it's all clear cut in driving. Driving is no metaphor for life, which isn't a journey as people suggest, more an irregular pattern of vomit left on a pavement. That's what I find.

By and by we come to our destination, one of those old fashioned shop/warehouses in a back street, alongside a timber yard, a motor factors and a double glazing contractors. It's not clear what the shop sells. Bill takes one box and I take the other two. We push straight past the trade counter and through to a rear office.

'All right, Murray, your order.'

'Bill?' Murray is a late middle-aged geezer with greased-back hair who looks as if he may once have been a rocker. The hair is quite thin and isn't best served by being slicked into place: skin is visible between the comb lines. 'What are you doing here?'

'What do you mean, Murray? It's your regular order.'

Bills' voice has a slight 'salesman' tinge to it, an offbeat jokiness that I haven't heard from him before – years of practice in cold calling and bigging up the client.

Murray looks temporarily taken aback. 'I've cancelled

the account.'

'What do you mean, "cancelled the account"? How long have I been supplying you here? Twelve years? Fifteen?'

'I don't know, Bill, I wouldn't have thought…'

'Fifteen years and I drove out all this way.'

'I gave you plenty of notice. Janice let you know. I told her to call you up.'

'Call? What call? I've never had a call.'

'Janice called you up. Janice…Janice…Janice?'

There's a long wait while we stand. Bill has put his box down, but I still have hold of mine. Even though they're not that heavy, they're too big to be comfortable. Nothing is comfortable just at the moment. Janice takes too long to arrive. She enters eventually with a new cup of coffee. I guess she's used to finishing what she's doing before she attends Murray's bidding. She sips at her drink and positions herself at the fourth corner of our arrangement. 'Bill.'

'Janice.'

'Bill says you haven't let him know about the amended account.'

'I've phoned up, but I couldn't get through.'

Bill is slightly red now. 'How hard did you try? You know the number.'

She sips calmly at her coffee once more. 'I should think I've phoned a dozen times; the last few times it didn't recognise the number.'

'Who've you phoned?'

'Maggie, of course.'

Maggie is one of the secretaries that Bill has let go, along with the rest of the staff. Only Mal remains. The extra phone lines were cancelled weeks ago to save money, but Bill can't admit to that. He's deep red now. He turns to Murray. 'If you want to cancel an order you talk to me, you talk to me.'

Murray's not happy about Bill's tone of voice, but I can see he's controlling himself, 'We've not cancelled the order, Bill, we've closed the account.'

A small pause. 'Why?'

'We've just gone with a different supplier.'

'What supplier?'

'A different supplier.'

'What different supplier?'

Murray thinks for a moment. 'That's confidential business information.'

Bill's turn to pause. He looks like thunder. 'We'll see about that.' He strides out through the door through which Janice entered a few moments ago. She stays where she is, but Murray goes after. I feel like I have to follow.

Beyond the door is a corridor, then double doors and out into a warehouse. By the time I get there, Bill and Murray have disappeared, but I can tell where they are by the commotion. Bill's running up and down the rows of shelves and boxes with Murray following on, offering benedictions such as 'what the fuck' and 'you're out of order'. I only catch up when Bill has come to a stop.

'These, yeah?' he says.

'That's'

'Yeah, these.'

The boxes look like ours, about the same size, the same colour, similar lettering and trade marks. Bill looks them over, looks to Murray, says, 'They're fakes.'

'They're no fakes.'

'They're fakes. I've been in this business for years. I've seen every type of sheath and packaging and every type of carton and I know what I'm looking at: they're fakes, they're not right, they'll burst, there's no spermicide in the lubricant, they'll make your cock burn.'

'So what, Bill, they're cheap, they're half the price of yours.'

That's it. Bill stares deep into Murray's face, a couple of seconds at most but a real fermata amidst the chaos. Then he turns and goes back the way he came at the same pace he came in. I follow, Murray follows me, back up the corridor, through the office where Janice is now sitting, sipping her coffee, back past the trade counter, Murray's voice small behind, 'Bill, your boxes!'

'Keep the fuckers, Murray, fucking keep them.'

I have to drive aimlessly for a while, until Bill's colour returns to normal and I feel like I can say something.

'All right, Bill?'

'What? All right.'

'Breakdown in communication and fakes, yeah?'

'Fakes.'

'Where from?'

'Osman. Osman supplies them, never him personally, but always one of his men.'

I can see Bill's business winding down. First, the corporate distributors with their flash modern vending machines opening up new consumer bases, internet ordering, direct importation from the Far East, pubs getting taken over by the chains, Bill gradually getting squeezed out with his old-fashioned flyers and telephone contact. Next, the stuff I used to deliver suddenly and irrevocably unattainable, Bill having to rely again on all the old business, dwindling, increasingly undercut, laying off staff and, finally, fakes flooding the market.

'Home?'

'No, we're not done yet.'

Nevertheless, we have to go some way back the way we've come, showing how wasteful our delivery trip has been, through towns and green spaces dull in the rain, left, right, straight on. Bill gives directions. I don't ask anything more. Osman is the bogeyman.

We arrive at a steel stockholders. Bill's back to his old self now. He reads a list to the counter guy. 'Four off three metre seventy-five by fifty box section, mild steel; six metres fifty by fifty angle mild steel; three square metre four mill chequer plate.'

The guy goes off. We wait silently until the stuff

arrives and we all help to load it into the van. The plate is heavy in its big sheets and the long box sections a little awkward to manoeuvre, but they fit very well onto the length of the load floor. Bill's calculating something in his head as we stack it all in.

Then we drive away. It's lunchtime, but no mention of food. I've observed that Bill isn't bothered about eating during the day unless he's at home. The metal stock rattles and crashes in the back of the van – a giant baby's rattle heard at great distance.

When we get back to the works Mal is waiting: another thing that hasn't been mentioned. He helps us unload with the same considered eye with which Bill oversaw the loading. They are in their element, brought up on ferrous metals, fire and Bessemer converters. We grow up with what we know, for them, giant presses, rollers and guillotines; for me punk rock, poetry and Restoration tragedy. We all end up in the same place with the same job in hand.

Mal's cleared a space by the wall. The works is mostly space now. When we're done he looks satisfied. There's no mention of what the steel's for. Everything is like this. The information arrives piecemeal and when it's necessary. I don't necessarily like it, but I don't get a say.

And then we're done for the day. I drive Bill back to the house and I'm free to sit in my cold flat imagining cock-burning condoms.

WAYNE

From Birmingham I made my way to Northamptonshire and the new property I'd sought out on the internet. I wanted to be new, so I called myself Wayne and bleached my hair. My eyebrows stayed dark. When I caught myself in the mirror I looked entirely unfamiliar, an incubus version of myself.

The big estate I'd found to hide myself within was one of those planned municipal developments put up sometime in the late Fifties or early Sixties, planned as an entire community. It was supposed to have five pubs, three schools and 'village' shopping areas. Perhaps there had even been a doctors' surgery and a dentist's. Three of the pubs were boarded up, the schools had been subsumed into bigger places a bus ride away and the shops had dwindled to a convenience store with a busy lottery franchise and a pizza/kebab place of dubious quality.

I thought there would be anonymity in such surroundings, but in these places everyone knows everyone else. There are gangs and territories, local influence and loose alliances based on family and common interests, head men and elders with whom no one messes and cocky young wankers pushing the boundaries. The economy turns at every level: hard working types, well-paid, underpaid and barely subsisting; dole wallers, generations on the sick; drug takers and drug suppliers, sneak thieves who'll evaporate anything that isn't tied down; many decent people trying to make it all work and down-and-out shit-kickers with no ambition other than to ruin it for everyone else. And me, of course

My place was a small semi with a toilet accessed via the rear porch, anaglypta'd walls and condemnable gas fires in the two reception rooms. I bought an electric blanket and stayed in bed too long in the mornings. Of the two pubs, I went to the one that showed the least sport on its big screens and drank lager so that I would appear less out of place. I still did. I've never thought I had an accent but it seems that it's more to do with the rhythms of your speech. I've long since cut down on my vocabulary. When you've come in from elsewhere people want to know about you. They wanted to know whether I was working undercover for the DSS or CID. They don't want to get to know you out of friendship: they want to know if you're a threat.

Sometimes women will want to get to know you because your unfamiliarity makes you exotic. You're not one of the tossers they know and hate from old, who won't talk to you when Sky Sports are on. The pub has the same set of people in all the time, except for weekend dinners. There are day people and night people and a few who do both day and night. I'm only a night person and only when I need to get out of the house. The women come up to you and ask you what you're writing in your little book, 'You taking notes for the social?' and you almost tell them that you're working through the quiz-word anagrams before you remember where you are and say it's your shopping list (*brain*, *bear*, *bearing*, then, and more likely, *bean*, *bran*, *grain* – for the balanced diet, *breasting,* yes, the nine letter!). 'You drink lager, do you? I like a Breezer.' Pause here. 'Would you like a Breezer now?' Then they're weighing up how many of these it will take before you've earned a trip back to theirs for a quick hand job as they won't give out too soon, because that would make them a slut, but this only happens at the weekend when it's party night and all the men are branded – D & G, Lacoste, Ben Sherman, DKNY, FCUK et al and can be selected on the colour of their shirt, no trainers, no leather jackets. But you don't want a hand job because it's all so one sided. You want the way it was with Dawn or, much further back, the closeness you experienced with Gail... and then you stop. Whichever way you go you can never go back. I am dead in all but name. My name is dead.

'Breezer, then?'

'Ta, don't go special though, you haven't finished yours yet.'

'No trouble.'

She'd love to take a look at your notebook just to make sure you're not from the social, as Sasha's really too young to be looking after Billy on her own but you said, if she stayed up and looked after him she could have a tropicana with extra spicy beef when you got back. But then, how do you balance that? There's the blond guy with the dark roots that might be coming back with you. What's he going to think when he sees the kids? Will he fork out for the pizza and can you pretend it's for you right up until the last minute, especially when you hate pineapple when it's not in a drink. He's coming back with the Breezer like a real gent. Slim – does he work out?

I spent days exercising. There was a gym, at least, if you got the right bus. The people were more upmarket over there, their perfumes more likely to have been sold by dedicated sales staff than market-stall traders, both men and women. I liked to look at the women, but they weren't so keen on me with my bleached hair and slightly mad eyes. I looked like someone who is just about to lose his temper or who chain smokes, even though I've never smoked in my life. On the estate that was a standard look for some people, but I'd had to work my way up to it.

I ate on a budget: beans, bran and grain. Not quite: lasagne, salad, economy packs of bell peppers, grilled fish on odd occasions, three day keemas or dahls, cheese, crackers and cured meats on demand. I never put on weight, I don't think my frazzled metabolism had the time.

With no future, there was nothing to work for, so I simply passed the time and watched my back. I couldn't sign on, because that would mean registering my particulars. I couldn't state my name or National Insurance Number in case there were people still looking for me. I couldn't make connections around me because even beneath the radar, perhaps especially so, people won't put up with you unless they know enough about you. They want to know who your friends are and where you've been and you can't tell them you've been inside or been abroad because they will know someone who's spent time in the same places and can check you out. No one likes a stranger.

I could see that my money wasn't going to last. Deductions add up. As the months passed I husbanded my resources ever more closely. You start off with high standards even if you are being frugal, but standards require fiscal backup and without it they're apt to slip. Entertainment goes first, followed by nights at the pub and all too soon your lasagne is the bulk bargain type in blue and white cardboard and you're wondering how many Breezers it takes to get a hand job whilst the kids eat pizza in the bedroom.

MONKEY

Strange things happen when you're not paying attention. It's because of the way things evolve in a subtle progression of changes. The years of being alone, of being lonely, have made me unrecognisable to myself. As time has passed I've lost the facility for socialising. I no longer have quick conversation, or friendly chit-chat, or a ready smile to hand. Those capacities have atrophied from lack of use. I imagine that, to other people, I come across as somewhat creepy: I am not quite human, more the professor's assistant in a nightmare horror. The experiment has gone wrong.

I exist sufficiently only to complete the most basic tasks: eating, drinking, occasionally taking Lauren to school, making small preparations for the job, which may or may not occur in some unformed future.

Each morning I wake with the images in my head. I try to shut them out, even though they don't form fully anymore. They are something suggested or glimpsed out of focus, like a half-memory from childhood that you can't decide is real or dreamed.

Sometimes the days draw out and I look forward to meals to break the monotony. I save myself from wine until it is late enough to give in and finally obliterate the chattering monkey in my head.

I can now perform half of the roof bars. I've read about training in the past, so I know that rest is an integral part of the process, but sometimes I will work out on the bars twice in a day. The second time is always compulsive and derives from that odd mental state that allows you to forget the pain of earlier events so that you can enjoy the brief rush of endorphins when you've finished. In the same way, but opposite, a hangover is the last thing on your mind when you settle in for a heavy session. It's probably an addiction, the exercise, and is the only thing that prevents me from stopping completely. I am astoundingly weary in a way that permeates all aspects of my existence. Fatigue has invaded every cell in my body and I am now sodden with it, weighed down. I drag myself from moment to moment by sheer willpower alone. Sometimes, at night, it catches up with me completely and I sit stupefied like the blank-faced sheep that can sometimes be seen at the edge of the garden.

Such a state of affairs takes years to concoct, years of solitary confinement in places with no telephone and no one to phone if you had one.

When I moved from Birmingham to my semi-detached in the east Midlands the only thing that improved was my immediate environment. There were no longer people in adjacent rooms snoring through the afternoon or signalling the final peaks of Onanism. On the other hand, there was nothing at all. I never met my neighbours. They never came round offering cake to welcome me to the neighbourhood. I am a weirdo and to be avoided. Something about me, I know, sucks the life from around me and kills it. Only the insensitive can put up with that kind of thing, which is why the boys don't notice. I guess I'm not unique.

I took walks from my house, firstly to get the lie of the land, eventually just for a change of scenery. Gradually, I stopped noticing where I was going. It was enough just to walk with no pleasure or purpose. If I was walking I wasn't spending money.

The estate in which I lived was supposed to be a self-contained community, but you had to go to town to do anything like go to the library, a soulless concrete structure built to the highest standards of Sixties modernist alienation. The rows of steel shelving cradled the books like objects of hate. I went in mostly to read the paper or read the paper whilst waiting interminable periods to get onto the internet. When I got onto the internet I didn't know what to do with it.

I could never get over my paranoia. When you parachute yourself into a community people inevitably take an interest. Every house has eyes; each eye is connected to a mind which wants to know what you are about.

I wound down my trips to the pub almost to a standstill. After a while the regular boys want to get you into conversation. They start you off on football, but your lack of interest means that you can't sustain the right level of banter. They talk about women, which is okay, but you can't talk about them in the same, predatory way. Their grasp of politics is slim, but held with overweening conviction. You end up on how shit life is on the social and the royal liberty of all the job interviews you're forced to take so that they don't take your benefit away. And you say 'too right' which leads inevitably to the 'what you do before then?' and 'what are you doing here?' and you respond with your well-rehearsed tales that you've made up for yourself that you would much rather believe than the actuality of your miserable history.

Truth is, you're a criminal and, in the thin instants between the waking state and bad dreams, you see people murdered in front of your eyes and dead bodies stripped of their souls in states of enforced rest. Unnoticed, your soul slipped away with them, forever, and you sit in the pub whilst real people, whatever their faults, try and buy you drinks and find out who you are. Simply, you are the undead, but that doesn't mean that you'd rather be dead, so you take their pissy lager and laugh about how unfair it all is while they pay for your drink with their untaxed income and you begin to think that this is the thin end of the wedge and right now someone is breaking into your social-housing semi-detached and rifling through your books of quiz-word solutions looking for clues. Soon it will be time to leave.

'So, who'd you work for again?'

'Motor factors' distributors in the stock room.'

'Any good?'

'Money was shit, but no one bothered you. All done on paper. Old fashioned. Then they got computers and that was it. Everything with these bin numbers, so they could lay off the more experienced, better paid men and bring in teenagers. Fucking liberty.'

'London, yeah?'

'Essex really, not far from Colchester.'

Good, now you won't be asking me about my home town and saying you once had a girlfriend there and what have they done to the shopping centre which I've never seen etcetera-fucking-etcetera...

I have never been tempted to share myself with anyone. The price I pay is to keep it all inside, which is why I've stopped going inside and why my waking days are experienced solely on a thin veneer of existence.

In all communities there are people with power, people operating on the black economy. These people most of all want to know what you're up to. They usually have a single name, which will come up every so often: 'Todd'; 'Mr Greaves'. A loner like me will always attract their interest, because I could be anything, a Police informant, an undercover officer. Of course, I'm under cover, but on the other side of the law. It makes you think that, eventually, they will find out about you. You don't know how they will manage this, considering that even your last outfit didn't really know who you are, but you're paranoid, so you figure that people will have their ways. So then you're looking over your metaphorical shoulder all the time. The mind feeds on itself when it's left to its own devices. It will eat what's available.

Before I could fully understand just what the endless mechanism of time had done to me, I was pushing two years on the run. The money was all but gone. In desperation I got on a bus that went over to some distant pub to find work, just as I had done years before and ended up working The Route, something which I never planned, nor anticipated. I'd remembered some twat in the local telling me that you could sometimes get cash-in-hand work that way. It's a black economy and it works underground.

So I ended up working for a building contractors, ripping out an old-fashioned department store so that it could be refitted as a modern minimalist boutique housing franchises for designer labels. I could just see how it was going to be, as we crowbarred out the period detail, from the Victorian staff toilets to the rows of Forties fire buckets, finally the false ceilings which hadn't done ten years, a source of great joy to those who knew the ropes and collected up the aluminium frameworks to weigh in for beer tokens at the scrap merchants.

The boys were either very young, and had taken work to keep the DSS off their backs, or in their mid fifties and probably been in the Lump for decades. Most of them seemed to have come from a few towns in County Clare and knew each other's workings to the nth degree.

Each night they went en masse to the one pub that would cash their cheques and drank until it was time to slink off back to their digs.

I was somewhere in between and, as usual, fitted in nowhere. The young ones thought I was an old man, so I stuck with the old men and saw what I could learn. There is an economy of effort in the practised hand: you don't look like you're getting anywhere quickly, but the results speak for themselves. In contrast the young fuckers blasted away at it and had less to show for it at the end of the day. Effort was what it was all about as, according to some, the contract had been underbid and there was less than no room for slack in the operation. So we worked like dogs. I paid attention, because I thought that this might be a way to go on, the itinerant workman, cash in hand where possible. That would keep me under the radar. I was also quite enjoying the activity, even if it meant that I had to lie on the floor stiff as a board at night. There was something akin to satisfaction in it but, of course, it wouldn't last.

MAL

Bill and I are with Mal at the works. In the clear space inside the loading bay we have sorted out our steel stock and put the four long members onto the floor. Bill has brought tools from my garage: a nine inch angle grinder, with assorted discs, a box of files, hacksaw and emery cloth. Mal has arrived with a fuck-off MIG welder, mask, wire brushes and all the rest.

We set to. There are no drawings, but both of them seem to know exactly what they are doing. There is a set routine. There are measurements. We get the four long, three metre lengths and lay them in two, closely spaced parallel pairs. Bill runs a tape between the paired members, making sure that they are exactly one foot apart all the way down. Next, the angle iron: Mal and I hold the 'L' section lengths hard to a bench and Bill cuts off one foot lengths with the angle grinder. The noise hurts my ears and the hot smoke assaults my nostrils. Sparks spray onto the floor, alive for an instant, cold and dead the next. The cut sections clatter as they drop onto the concrete, bright wounds from the cut marks serried with burr teeth, hot in the mouth. My ears ring even after the grinder shuts off. Bill and Mal don't seem to notice. Metal is their element. I belong to the fluidity of motion, driving, weaving through traffic on a bike. This is addressing the human will to hard objects, breaking down their natural resistance with overwhelming force. Bill and Mal are stone-faced. They proceed as if the whole process is fixed and merely waits to unfold under the application of their will.

We pick up the eighteen new lengths and file away the burrs between the three of us. Toothless now, they are distributed between the two pairs of long box sections, seven linking each pair with four left over. Bill measures the spacing exactly from figures inside his head.

The rectangular box sections are shorter edge down with the long sides perpendicular to the floor. The angle iron links sit on the floor with their ninety-degree ridges uppermost, like little roofs extending between the two long members. Mal fires up the MIG while I hold the connecting bars in place in turn. I have a thick leather gauntlet. I can't look at what I am doing: the arc is too bright to look at. Mal has a mask. When I look back new weld secures the sections together. We work down one side and back up the other. This is easier, as the links are solidly attached to one of the long members. All I have to do is put my foot against the long member to stop it moving away. Time goes, burnt metal fills the air, the high voltage arc lights up the four corners of the works blue, throwing spider shadows leaping from the empty shelving units. I smell testosterone.

It's a long time since I've slept with a woman – far

too long for someone of my proclivities – and that was just someone I met in a pub in Birmingham, some place that I'd walked out to just for a change. The long walk had made me thirsty, so I drank too quickly. The trick is to drink water first to slake your thirst and then move onto beer. They'll give you water if you buy a beer at the same time.

The place was quiet at first, but by half nine there was loud music and scores of people. Saturday night – I had long since lost track of the days. It transpired that there was dancing in another room. Young women dressed in next-to-nothing came and went at the bar; men in untucked, patterned shirts and sports watches milled around with drinks in bottles; I sat at my corner table alone with my pints of Stella. The night progressed rapidly and it became too late for me to move on somewhere else. Two men and four women sat at the table next to me and started talking about reality – they'd seen it on TV. A girl across at the bar stood with her back to me, bare shouldered with a single spaghetti strap defining the line of her neck. As she moved her arms to complete the transaction the muscles made soft shapes in her pale skin. Her back tapered to her waist. I sucked my beer mindlessly. The music was now thumping with bass from the unseen room, the bar heaving and me taking an entire table to myself. The girl with the back turned round just in time to see me watching her with my bleary eyes.

Sometime after twelve I heaved myself out onto the

street. Maybe it was later. There were people everywhere. I hadn't taken in when I arrived that there were several pubs and clubs in close proximity. There was some kind of changeover taking place – some were closing, others coming into their own, massed hordes migrating to the next watering hole, much whooping and harr-ing, throwing up and stumbling about, me a solitary shambling island in a sea of hedonism. All couples and groups, the palpable scent of sexual intent oozing from a billion pores on every side, predatory packs seeking something out, two girls walking up and down looking at every unattached man in the street. How did I get so old? Which way did I come? A hand on my arm.

'All right?'

There was a woman beside me, thirty something, doe-eyed make-up, a slight sheen of perspiration showing through her silvery blush.

'Yeah, all right.'

She looked at me without removing her hand: claimed.

'I seen you sitting in the corner. You not got a girlfriend?'

How very forward. 'Not tonight.'

'Did yow see me over by the bar?'

No. 'Yes.'

'You're not from here. Do you live local?'

'Not quite.' My head was spinning a bit. Her lipstick had something pearlescent about it. Both of us way too drunk.

‘I’ve been left on my own and I haven’t got any money left for a taxi. We could share one.’

Actually, I’d been fully intending to walk back to the doss house and pass out. I’d long outstayed my welcome and it was too cold for us to be standing around. I had my leather jacket on, but her bare shoulders were showing goose pimples, her heat radiating away in the night air.

Her house had one bedroom, a small house in a newly built close of starter homes. Divorced, I thought. There were no pictures of any ex-husbands, but a sense of newness in the soft furnishing which suggested a relatively recent split. She brought me brandy in a green balloon. I would have been better off with a coffee or something. We didn’t say too much other than an exchange of names and ‘Nice place, how long have you been here?’ before she was transferring her lipstick onto my wet mouth. She tasted of brandy and smelled of make-up and eau de cologne. I tried to stop my head spinning.

In the bedroom she made an odd, urgent grunting sound as we kissed, more so when I was inside her. It felt strange, but I was too drunk for self-analysis. Something basic and animal was going on, her clothes strewn on a bedroom chair and mine on the floor. Half way through I had to go for an unscheduled piss and caught the reflection of my naked form in the bathroom mirror for the first time in years – something of a shock.

The house was hot, the bedroom almost stuffy as we worked our way up an inevitable conclusion. My sweat ran with the bitter smell of hops.

We performed once more after an interlude of half sleep. She kept her eyes closed and I wondered, in my oversoaked way, whether she was picturing her ex-husband or options one, two or three from earlier in the evening before she settled on me as an emergency last-ditch choice. I thought of no one. I don't remember anyone else to think about. I occupy a world of me, but not for preference: I don't really like it there.

Morning was far too early for drunks. When I returned from my trip to the bathroom she was sitting up in bed covering her breasts with the sheets, even though I'd covered them with semen just a few hours before. She looked at me making a sorry exhibition of myself in her bedroom. Both of us thought through the motions of the coming hours, the mechanics of washing, towels, breakfast, explanations. I walked towards her a step. She pulled the sheets tighter around her bosom. What must I look like? A doss-house surfer with a bag of ill-gotten cash under the bed, someone without friends, relatives, connections, a place in society, even the slightest hint of a direction. Now I saw the walls with their contract magnolia and the budget pine bedroom suite, by the side of the bed a spring exercise thing to stave off aging, the tidy white doors of the fitted wardrobe and the pink hairdryer sitting on the dressing table. I was older than she by some way, I guessed, and way outside the precincts of my tiny world. I would have liked a shower, but I started to pull on my clothes, over my sticky form.

‘You going?’

‘Yeah, got to go to work.’

‘On Sunday?’

Hmm. ‘Yeah, I have to work Sundays: I’m an undertaker.’

Her expression of distaste mixed with one of relief that I was going. Perhaps I was being cruel, but it was simply the first job that came into my head. None of this was right. It even overwhelmed my hangover. I wondered whether it would be right to cross over and kiss her farewell and ‘thanks’ or ‘commiserations’ or whatever, but in the event I just turned round and fucked off.

Now we had two long ladders laid out on the works floor. Bill had been busy marking out the big sheets of chequer sheet with their patterned grip surface. They’re heavy when we lift one onto a bench and shuffle it along to create an overhang. Bill addresses the angle grinder to an edge and commences to cut off a strip a little over a foot wide. It’s tough stuff and the grinder runs forever, spinning sparks in huge showers. The grinding numbs the ears; the vibration through the sheet plays a note through your body, right through to your soul.

Mal and I circulate around the sheet holding it in different positions to facilitate the cutting. Without being asked, I get hold of the free end of the piece that’s being cut off to stop it sagging. I'm good at this sort of thing. I know what people want from me without being told. I can detect it and just get on with it. I'm one of life's natural assistants. Heat from the cutting disc radiates down the plate to my hands. It all takes time. One strip follows another. We don't talk much. We keep to one task at a time – good production practice: keep like-tasks together to reduce change and unnecessary movement, stay with the same tool until it's time for the next operation.

We tidy up the sheets with files and emery cloth and lay them on top of the two ladders to form complete surfaces. They cover them exactly except for half an inch at one end.

This time Mal tacks them on with short stitches of weld rather than continuous runs. It's all rather neat and orderly and cuts down the time. We've been working all afternoon and it's dark outside – sparks in the dark.

There are four spare sections of chequer plate in our standard width, but shorter. I've been wondering about these. I see Bill taking a moment's thought. He goes over to a shelf and picks up a couple of pieces of redundant chewing-gum machine. At one end of our fabrications he places a section of chequer plate angling down onto the floor, at the other he places another kicking up into the air. He supports it manually at what I take to be the ideal angle, the same as the angled down piece at the opposite end, supports it with a piece of machinery, adjusts it a couple of times to get it right, refers to the opposite end and lets Mal get on with seam welding the two new sections onto the existing run of plate.

One of the remaining pieces of angle iron goes underneath the plate at each end to reinforce it and triangulate it onto the main run of the box sections. Mal tacks them on and we turn the whole thing over so that he can get it cobbed up to his satisfaction. Then it's straight onto the other unit to duplicate the process.

We haven't as much as sniffed a cup of tea all afternoon. I stink of burnt iron. We finish the job without even a look back at the finished product. It's just a step on the way and not a cause for celebration or emotion. There are few emotions nowadays, just fleeting whispers that remind you that emotions once existed, along with other fine things. Don't think about anything; keep your nose to the grindstone.

We wash our hands in cold water and Vim, which abrades the skin. Mal's beginning to look shaky. I know why that is.

'We away for a drink then, Bill?'

'I'm taking Justine and Lauren out for dinner.' He looks at his watch. I guess he'll be needing the car. He hasn't told me anything about it, but why should he?

'John?'

I don't really relish the thought of spending a night out with Misery Mal reliving the privations of his divorce. I could easily settle into my garage pad, soak in the aubergine bath and fix myself something to eat. I wouldn't mind some quiet to enjoy the musical ringing in my ears. I could sleep early, rise early and get swinging around the garage for the good of body and mind. I'm too scruffy to go out and I'm sure that whatever boozery Mal has in mind is going to be less than receptive to a nancy southern pooftah like me. Bill's on his way back to the house anyway, to pick up the rest of his family, so all in all it's a done deal. 'All right, Mal, let's get a fucking drink.'

JACK

I feel tension in the group. These are easy-going criminals, not troubled by inconvenient notions of conscience. They're not too hot on consequences either. I've wondered about this many times watching the news and reading the papers. These tragedies: a young woman abducted and raped, rotting in a ditch a month later. Doesn't the perpetrator ever employ their imagination? An act like this adds nothing to anyone: a life is cut short, all its aspirations, history, present, future, snatched away for nothing more than transient reasons; family, friends, acquaintances, their lives never quite the same again, always for the worse; the public purse suffering from the vast expense of investigating, prosecuting and accommodating the guilty in prison. Is the perpetrator better off? No, their quality of life has nosedived on every level from the minute to the global. I don't care if you're a sociopath or a psychopath, it's not to do with an inability to empathise or overwhelming desires or whatever, if you can read or watch TV or listen to the radio, then you'll have heard countless accounts of this sort of thing, turned over and analysed in the minutist detail. It's simply a matter of imagination – take any one of these highly publicised scenarios, place yourself in the appropriate place in the picture and see how it would turn out for you. Then, when you're ready to set out on your murder spree, don't bother.

The tension between the boys is a kind of pre-match thing. They're about to perform. So far it's all been preparation; in time it will be execution, even if we don't know when yet. They're worried about coming up short in the face of the others. I feel it myself. It creates tension. Euan and Deep almost had a stand-up fight over nothing in the Waverley until Bill intervened with a, 'Calm down, boys, you're making twats of yourselves.'

No one needs extra attention. I've often wondered about all this socialising at the pub, a bunch of guys with a purpose out without their other halves. We don't whisper, but we don't talk too loud. We look like a conspiracy. But then, who else in the Waverley is on with their own, clandestine business? What about the two old geezers in the corner? One was probably a cat burglar in his youth and the other a gangland enforcer. They've just retired in old age to raise pigeons. The middle-aged woman with the walking cane? She must have run an escort service up in the city before being shut down one too many times. So they probably don't care what we're up to.

Where are the Police in all this? I've never figured that out. Our whole, sublime economy potters on without reference to them. Euan and Deep never mention them, except for the odd tale about troublesome punters at whatever club. They've been dealing and robbing and passing dubious goods around for year on year without being collared. Only Mal's been inside, and that was years ago because he was a career criminal and because he's probably too stupid not to have left fingerprints and hair samples, footprints and his Blockbuster membership card at the scene of crime.

'What, officer? Not me.'

'Malcolm, you left your passport and your mother-in-law at the premises. She phoned you in as a missing person.'

Activity follows quiet. We are waiting for the next phase of the job. I am waiting, because other members of the team have real jobs to get on with. I don't like it. I'm weary when I come to rest. When I'm moving I don't notice – driving Lauren to school, bringing her back, running errands for Bill, getting a few things at the shop. Only when you are still do consequences catch up with you. Perhaps that's how the rapists and murderers feel: when they're at it they're happy; after it's done they just want to be happy again.

I am with Deep and Euan in the car. Most activities set out with a journey. It's Euan's car, though he seems to have got rid of the Evo and moved onto a newer BMW coupe in fetching silver. It's more of a squeeze in the back for me and I don't like being a passenger at the best of times.

We do things in separate groups. Mal and Bill have been shopping for tools; Bill and I have wandered far and wide picking up oddments of clothing. Perhaps Euan and Deep have their own tasks, but so far I've not been privy to them.

This trip is personal business. It has something to do with the fallen-through deal on that batch of Euan's trainers. He hasn't told me much more. Euan's driving the new car through territory with which I'm not familiar. Not understanding the codes of practice for interpersonal criminal support adds to my feeling of being out of place. It's all implicit.

It's quite a good neighbourhood. The parked cars we're driving past have moved upmarket. I would call it up-and-coming, if not already risen, suburban semi-detached, middle-class aspirant (or arriviste), probably built up in the Twenties or Thirties, houses for the masses that probably cost a bundle even here.

'Over here, Euan, left down here.'

Evidently they're seeking somewhere they haven't been before. It's been more than a week since the guy failed to turn up for the trainers and I guess he's taken some finding.

'That's it.'

Business proceeds upon the slightest connection. It's all about those with spare money being put in touch with something they're willing to pay for. Sometimes there are intermediaries; sometimes the buyer never even meets the seller. Everything can be commoditised, from stolen credit card details to a young woman's existence.

Perhaps there are patterns in this, fractal progressions within the apparently chaotic and endlessly interlinked morass of micro deals and macro movements of goods, cash and services. No one sees more of the picture than that which is directly ahead of them, not even me, with the perspective of the permanent outsider.

We go a little way past our target and park in a side street. Euan is very protective about his car, placing it carefully next to the kerb in a slow-motion, parallel-parking manoeuvre that keeps two or three cars waiting even in a quiet street like this. So much for keeping a low profile.

They're not huge blokes, but they spend a lot of time in the gym, countless man months of bashing away on the machines and doing ill-advised sit-ups with weights. I pity their mashed discs, but they do look right, with their triangular backs and square shoulders.

It's a pleasant little place with a crimson door. We've arrived a little after five, so there's a good chance he'll be home. Three men at the door. Euan knocks even though there's a bell. The door opens, a woman, maybe thirty-five, pale hair, almost blonde.

'Can I help you?'

'We're here to see Ken.'

She looks uncertain. I can see her thinking. She doesn't like the look of it, but she can't justify closing the door. She doesn't want to be stuck here facing us. She is weighing up all she knows about Ken, about their long term commitment to each other, the quality of their relationship, what she suspects she doesn't know. Her head turns slightly back towards the house and her route of departure, it returns to us, turns back again.

'I'll just fetch him.' For her the solution is to move the question on to someone else. 'Ken, it's for you.'

As soon as she has moved away we step over the threshold, just enough to be inside without invading the personal space of the house. We fill the narrow hall.

Ken arrives with a question mark on his face, 'Who...?'

'Euan'

'Ah. What do you want?'

He's a little defiant, asserting himself as master of his domain.

'What d'ya think? I want my money for my trainers.'

'For the trainers? No. I did another deal. That money's gone.'

'Is it, now? Did you not understand? A deal's a deal where I come from.'

'Well, I got a better deal somewhere else. That's done.'

'Who with?'

'That's my business?'

'No, that's MY business.'

'Well it's done and that's it, so perhaps you'd like to be on your way.'

'All right, we'll be away then. Next time you see any of your mates, tell them that it's fine to make a deal with Euan and break it off at your own convenience.'

There's a subtle shift in Ken's demeanour. The eye contact has gone. He's looking more at Euan's chin.

'We'll put it down to experience, eh?'

'Oh, it'll be an experience all right.'

Deep has closed the door behind us. It's crimson on the inside too.

'Stella, Stella, why don't you see to wee Jack upstairs?'

Stella appears at the kitchen door with a tea towel. 'You what, Ken? What do these gentlemen want?'

'Go upstairs and see to Jack.'

'I'm not going anywhere until you tell me what's going on with these men. Are they from your team?'

If anything, we play for an opposing side.

Ken half turns to Stella. Any mellowness in his voice has turned to anger. 'Stella, do what I fucking tell you and get up the stairs and see to wee Jack now.'

She evidently hasn't been spoken to like this for some time. 'I will not. Now tell me what's going on.'

That's quite enough for Euan. He moves down the hall and closes on Ken. Deep and I follow on.

'With me, sunshine.' He grabs Ken by the shirt. Ken's about middling height and maybe thirteen stone - stout without being over fat - but Euan has him off his feet in a second and is dragging him up the hall towards an open door to our left. Ken struggles. Deep has him now, by one of his legs, and the whole mass proceeds in ungainly fashion up the remainder of the hall and through the doorway via much contact with the frame.

Stella is screaming. She's screaming words, but I can't identify any of them. I look her in the eye for a moment, before I follow into the living room. She looks surprised as much as upset, something has upset her world. The first thing I see in the living room is her wedding picture, where it's has been knocked off a side table. She is close behind me. We enter almost as a couple. Ken is on the floor and Deep has one of his legs held up in the air. The other is thrashing about. Blood is pouring from his nose and one of his eyebrows. He looks less like Ken now.

'Get his fucking leg, John, get it.'

'No, leave him alone, leave him alone,' These words of Stella are more clear.

I get the other fucking leg, which is none too easy. He kicks me in the chest first off and narrowly misses my face. There's a method to this. I follow Deep's lead and pull the leg up into the air and apart from the other. Ken flounders on the ground waving his arms around uselessly. Stella has moved to hitting Deep on the back. It does less than nothing. Euan steps up and pushes her over. She bounces over the arm of the settee and onto the floor, dazed.

'Right Ken, you don't think a deal's a deal, do you?' He moves between Ken's legs with his bouncer's fist and punches directly down into his knackers. 'D'ya ken now?'

Do you ken, Ken? The scream is more high-pitched even than Stella's. Ken's arms stop thrashing. I'm holding onto his leg really tight as he tries to double up.

'Who'd you do the deal with? Who? Who'd you do

the deal with?'

High pitched again, 'Dougie, Dougie, you know, Dougie.' He's out of breath.

'You fucking cunt.' Euan's big fist backs up right into his shoulder and shoots down a second time into Ken's gonads. The scream is ear-piercing. Every neighbour in the district must be able to hear. Perhaps that's part of the desired effect: maximum impact. Ken is crying. His legs have gone slack. Deep and I drop them at the same instant, without reference. Stella is trying to get off the floor. She looks upset, really, really upset. Her face merges with the image I have of her happy, in the wedding photograph.

Euan leans over to Ken, 'Don't you ever, ever, let me fucking see you again, all right?'

Nothing.

'ALL RIGHT?'

'Aye.' A tiny, strangled voice.

Everything about me is attenuated. I am more solid than before. My hearing has focused down into this small space around me. Our breath – the three of us who have paid the visit – has thickened the atmosphere of the room. It's humid and hot. Dust motes from the disturbed furnishings intermingle with the exhaled mist of snot and saliva. Whatever happens here from now on, the room will never be the same again.

'Let's get the fuck out of here.'

We turn to go. Wee Jack is at the living room door. I guess he's been there for some time. We leave the front door open as we leave the premises.

'Dougie?' asks Deep.

'Aye, he's something to do with Osman.'

LAUREN

Here's a thing: the past poisons the present. Each incremental error adds to the others to create your state of affairs. No single decision makes it so, no schedule or contract, simply the sum total of your past failures in all their fractured glory.

It's too late to make good. Now the curtains are a little closed and the room darker. I don't see the final details so much. The infinite blue sky in the landscape framed above the fireplace looks flat and grey in this light. Each night I go to sleep alone in my single bed and stay awake into the early hours unless I have completely obliterated myself with alcohol. Some day I will lie down for a long rest.

Each morning I awake and rebuild myself from scratch. I have limited form, so it doesn't take long. Much of it is to do with clothes. Naked, I am a ghost; in my casual but workmanlike outfit I am a semblance of human.

I drink coffee and wash up my few things, mismatched plates from history, a pink melamine mug, things left behind by a previous tenant. I swing from the bars, I float in the bath, I look along myself as I have done since I was a boy. I massage my head with the shampoo, imagining rigs and furrows of tension beneath my fingertips.

I change my clothes as often as I can. Because then I can go up to the house and ask to do the laundry. It is my one stipulation that I do this myself rather than let Justine do it: it's too personal.

The washing machine has a fast cycle. I don't use this. It's too optimistic. The machine washes better when it takes three times as long and I'm happier when I can spend three times longer in the house. Here is the only bright place to sit, in front of the washing machine in the utility watching every movement of my few clothes as they fold and fall, drown and spin.

The first thing that goes when you have no resources and no real life are favourable environments. No friends, no friends' homes, no dinner invitations, no social outings to the cinema or theatre, no pub afterwards for G-and-Ts and post-act analysis. No bar mitzvahs, christenings or piano recitals. No netball match and no table for eighteen at Pizza Hut. The only vestigial hint of these things afforded to me is these brief intervals in the family home, with its pristine plasterwork and fitted units – Bill's palace. Everything has been about this, from the prophylactic business to the dealer network to the carousel fraud. Each small increment a step on the path to this house and a consummate lifestyle for Lauren and Justine.

I try to commence the washing at about 4pm. Soon afterwards, if she's not doing girl stuff at one of her friend's, Lauren will turn up. Justine is a fresh-faced, attractive woman, but Lauren sparkles. She doesn't realise this and I wonder whether I overestimate it – I don't get out much.

Today, Lauren has come home. She hoves into the adjacent kitchen with a sigh that I know indicates a hankering for food. She eats a lot. I've seen her. If she snacks now it will be a plateful. It won't affect dinner later. Her meals provide an energy which radiates into the dark corners of my soul.

She has no conception that a one can sit with an approximation of contentment in front of a washing machine for one hour and thirty-seven minutes. That way lunacy lies though, apparently, you can spend an entire night watching numpties go about meaningless tasks in some reality show, even when you're round at a friend's with all the opportunities of mateship at hand.

'Hello, John. What are you doing?'

'My washing.'

'How can you do that? Just watching it going round for hours.'

'I'm a bit dim. It makes me easily pleased.'

'You're worse than dim, John, you're mental. Why don't you have the radio on or something at least?'

We've had conversations like this before. 'The radio interrupts the voices from the machine.'

She looks uncertain, but I am smiling slightly, I think. 'They're not telling me to do bad things, they're just grumbling about the weather.'

Today she wears a blue school sweatshirt and a knee-length skirt. I guess there are rules about such things. She puts her shoulder bag on the counter and props herself up against the dryer. I lift my head from my hands and lean back into my chair.

'What don't they like about the weather?'

'That it's not drying weather.'

I look for signs of the omnipresent drizzle in Lauren's hair. Probably she has walked just a couple of steps from the car to the door. There is a green tint in her blue eyes, looking at me.

'I think you should get out more. Hasn't Dad got you doing something?'

'By and by, a little bit here, a little bit there.'

'What sort of thing? He doesn't tell us anything about it.'

'Not much, just a sort of project down at the works, loose ends kind of thing.'

'Mum's worried about this. She thinks we're going to go bankrupt and have to sell the house.'

'There's not much chance of that.'

'But Dad's let all the staff go, Mable and everybody.'

'There's still Mal.'

'Uh, don't. I used to have to call him Uncle Mal. He's such a tosser.'

'That's men for you.' I, too, am a tosser.

'Dad's not like that.'

'No, he's a stand-up geezer.'

'You make me laugh.'

‘Why?’

‘Because you’re so southern and out of place round here. Why haven’t you got a proper job somewhere else? I reckon Dad makes up stuff for you do. It can’t be right living in that skanky garage.’

‘I told you, Lauren, I’m not very bright. For a good job you have to either work hard or be intelligent or both. Because I’m a bit lazy I’m stuffed and because I didn’t work hard at school I don’t have what they call transferable skills, which is why YOU have to work hard through your exams so that you can go off to university and proper, gainful employment. It’s either that or marry a footballer.’

‘No, don’t, it’s revision time and I’ve had to get the whole thing planned into a diary. There won’t be any free time left for living and today we were fucking around in English on something that isn’t even a set text for context or something, some play set in the French revolution by Peter Wise or something.’

‘Weiss: *The Persecution and Assassination of Marat as Performed by the Inmates of the Asylum of Charenton under the direction of the Marquis de Sade.*’

‘Fuck me, John, how did you know that?’

‘Just a lucky guess.’

She shakes her head at me in disbelief. I believe I am now grinning. I have her foxed. She’s right that I’m out of place.

‘So I suppose you couldn’t tell me anything about Coleridge and Wordsworth then.’

'Romanticism and the transcendent glory of nature? Never heard of it.'

'You're teasing me, you bastard.'

'No, I told you, if I knew anything I'd have a pukka job with all the trimmings.'

Her hands are resting on the edge of the surface and she's relaxed a little. I'm leaning further back into my hard chair and our physical relationship is a kind of triangle formed by our interconnected gaze and our angled bodies with feet just a few inches apart. For the duration of our conversation the washing has been going through the motions of its final spin quite quietly: it's a quality machine. Now it comes to rest and I realise I've missed part of the show. Even though the sound had not been intrusive, the silence provides a major change. I'm all self-conscious now. Lauren is unchanged. The way her nose ends with the beginning of her clear forehead would take me to another place if I had left the means by which to travel. So much for the Romantics and the transcendency of Nature, how about washed up in a pointless existence tossed around by malevolent forces? I am just a few inches from Lauren, separated by a whole lifetime of shit, disappointment and self-recrimination.

She's waiting for me to speak. The machine beeps impatiently, telling me it's stopped and 'please empty my belly.' Lauren hasn't had her snack yet. I'm hungry as well. Watching the washing always makes me hungry, like vicarious swimming. This is one of those longing moments, stretching out further than their allotted time, stealing something of the next moment, eating it and growing fat.

The machine beeps again. I've never heard it beep twice. I always empty it as soon as it's beeped its first. However long those seconds are, as soon as we get to six, someone will have to speak. This is how long studies have shown that people can bear silence in a conversation.

Six. 'Why don't you come and have something to eat in the kitchen, John?'

Why don't I? Justine keeps a packed fridge. Why don't I sit down with Lauren and talk through her revision notes, see if I can add anything worthwhile? I haven't sat with someone young in more than forever, in the primordial dark before the big bang. Having a snack might mean another hour in the warmth of the house with the sounds of other people moving between rooms and getting on with the business of life. But last evening I went with the boys round to Ken's family home where I helped them smash him up in front of his wife and wee Jack. So, even though I'd love to bathe in Lauren's unalloyed effervescence. I cannot reconcile the two things together.

'Sorry, Lauren, I have a whole night's paperwork to do back at the flat.'

Even when it's just last night, the past poisons the present.

KIDS

Later, I am alone in my room. Bill and Justine are hosting guests for dinner. They do this once a week at least. I am never invited. Bill likes to keep things separate. Even though I live in the garden, I belong to a tawdry world of graft and the ill-gotten. Justine and Lauren have to be kept away from that as much as is humanly possible. On the surface it might seem to be a mental accommodation of incompatibilities, but I know from experience how you can justify almost anything to yourself if you think needs must, if the rewards are high enough. You simply stifle the imagination. We have a limitless capacity to explain away our shortcomings. I, with my academic background, simply employ more sophisticated excuses.

There are two chairs at my kitchen table. My flat seems like a holiday home from another era. It has seen better days. Tonight's meal consisted of the second half of a cheap beef joint masquerading as steak that I started last night and the same array of vegetables. In these circumstances I will drink an entire bottle of my budget red, but I stop there even if I feel like going on. Sometimes I sit at the table for a long interval after I have finished eating, drinking from my sole Paris goblet in a slight semblance of being civilised. Drink is dessert. I don't bother with any other sort. I look at the empty seat opposite me in silence. This is the methodology of carving up the day, making finite chunks out of the unformed expanse of time. I have cooked twice today; I have watched two films; I have swung on the bars. Even now my deltoids are complaining of the strain...

The bottle is gone or, rather, it remains, empty. I have sat for an hour. An hour stands for any indefinite, but long, period of time. I think of them up at the house, laughing. Justine cooks well. Lauren is a passable help if she can drag herself away from her fashion magazines.

The curtains are always open, even at night. How many times I've ridden past lit windows on my bike, those split-second snapshots of warm rooms and lives going on in comfort as the wind whistled around my visor, each interior a story with its own cast and drama of human interaction. Even now, stationary in my own apartment, I am passing by in the dark while it all goes on elsewhere, the ticking of the heart the ticking of the bike's slick tyres on the tarmac…

Something has entered the silence, a slight ruction in the field. Nothing close, but not too far away. I don't hear it as much as detect a miniscule deviation in the run of my thoughts. It's late, and it's not the dinner guests leaving: they're drinking and staying over. It's Saturday, I think. Is it? More noise. Odd to feel that you can judge the size of an animal by the form of its sound. This animal? Large. I wait until the noise recedes in memory and transforms itself to myth. I haven't moved from my chair, but now I am listening. Nothing. Something. There is someone outside.

I feel odd moving so slowly through my own domain. I am conscious of my own sound. I cross quietly to the door at the top of the stairway, open it and pass through to the gantry. Below, the cars are quiet in the darkness. The Audi a grey slab; Justine's Mini a brief pale punctuation of cream roof. Have never as much as heard a mouse in this space before. I listen into very corner in turn. It takes time. I am alone in the garage: I'm sure of that.

The wooden stairs are impossibly squeaky as I descend, one step at a time, unnaturally lowering myself from tread to tread as if they were feet apart. All the time I listen. I feel I hear a motion beyond the main doors, a brushing past or pressing against for the briefest moment. I reach the floor and head towards the personnel door at the side. It's never locked when I'm at home.

Outside it's cold and damp. I haven't, of course, put on a jacket and I'm just in my dark shirt. The stillness felt inside is betrayed by the external reality. Here is the ubiquitous fine mist of drizzle that has haunted me ever since I came north. A slow, cold wind pushes it into the folds of my shirt. Sounds, sub-articulated rushes of breath heard at a distance: there's more than one of them.

I have never thought too much about the garden. It's not somewhere in which it's been possible to spend time. When the plot was redeveloped it must have been razed along with the old house. There are just a couple of mature trees and one or two beds of shrubbery towards the boundaries. The rest is a vast sea of grass with sundry dwarf conifers and ornamental firs, all for ease of maintenance.

There's huge extent of dark and endless possibilities for cover. My garage is down in one corner of the grounds; the house stands above it on the opposite corner. The drive sweeps down from the front of the house in an aristocratic arc, with a diversion off to the garage. There must be more than a hectare of land all told. Light radiates from the windows of the house, but not far enough to light me. I wonder if the guests are having the grand tour of the house. Bill likes giving them the tour.

My targets are here, somewhere. They were together then, because they spoke. Are they now apart? I move swiftly away from the garage and out behind to the unoccupied corner, taking myself rapidly away from my start point, and theirs. When seeking prey, make sure you are outside their sphere of awareness. I remember this from way before. I look back towards the garage and then the house and wait for signs as my eyes gradually adjust to the level of light. It's moonless, starless and wet. Clouds are transferring to the ground in droplets and I'm shivering for more than one reason.

One of the square beams of light from the house flutters: movement inside. A light goes off downstairs and another comes on in the kitchen. For a moment I see him, a disembodied face by a fir, drawn back into the dark in an instant. Imperceptibly, I move from my spot and along the rear boundary towards the house. Beyond the fence is pasture and nothing else for a mile or more and the village. I think ahead. They will be mobile too. The hunter must always be wary of happening upon the quarry too quickly and being seen, so I slide through the darkness as smoothly as I can, paying intimate attention to what's coming up. The kitchen light goes off and the pattern has changed once more. I guess they've thought again and are keeping away from traps. Then, they don't know that I'm behind them.

I have traversed the entire rear boundary to the corner behind the house, carefully, using all the available cover. Between myself and the windows of the house fall the dark shadows of trees, contrasting with the light of the patio. There are a thousand places to remain concealed. Now I am low to the ground. My hands are wet and my shirt is sticking to my back. I move from cover to cover, making sure I am out of the lightest areas at all times. I feel that they are together now, closer to the house so, gradually, gradually, I close in. I watch. I wait

I am alone in the dark and suddenly overcome with an urge to stop the nonsense and identify the beast. I could rush up pronto and flush them out of the undergrowth or

I could simply run around like a stabbed rat, soaking wet, making a scene for Bill and the assembled guests. Then, before I can act, there's movement in the dark. Footfall? Ripples in the firmament. I look, sense. They are gone from behind the house. It's clear. I prick up my ears and hear. Through the drizzle. The doors of a car. Somewhere in the road. Up. Out. On. I stretch my long legs into stilts and run giant strides in a huge arc, around the house, beyond the reach of lightfall. My feet crunch the gravel as I leave the grass and cross the drive. I'm way too late. The car grinds off in a chatter of mechanics, a small, asthmatic engine and tin exhaust, some cheap, shit-heap hatchback. Things I recognise from the road, petty little teenage criminals in their chariot having a gander at the big house to see if there's anything to boost. They wouldn't like to get on the wrong side of Bill. When I was a teenager crime didn't feature on my radar; now there are petty fucking criminals in every sweaty nook and cranny, including the wretched crevice occupied by me.

I'm slightly out of breath and comprehensively wet. The journey back across the drive is slower and quieter. I'm keen to get back to the comparative warmth of my lodging, to take off my wet clothes and dry my hair with my spare towel. The other is wet from my bath earlier. Wet twice in one evening. The garage sheds little light, a thin grey wash from one of the windows, borrowed light from the door to my flat at the top of the stairs. No one lives there. They just exist. I'm not sure whether I'm shivering from the cold or from the exertion. The wise thing to do would be to go home but, instead, I re-track to the back of the house. The garden feels barren now, without drama.

I find my way to the same small fir where I thought I saw one of the watchers. I won't be telling Bill about it. There isn't much to tell and I don't want to add to his worries with everything that's coming up. Kids drive around all the time looking for opportunities, in between shooting up and vandalising property, hooting in the street and pissing in bins, it seems.

I'm just outside the light when Lauren comes into the kitchen. It must be the weekend if she's up this late. She reaches up into a cupboard and brings down a tin of something. She reads the label, puts it back and brings down another. This one seems to be right and, all too soon, she is gone from view and back to the party.

I'm gone from being wet to being soaked. A rivulet proceeds coldly down the crack of my behind. Light and dark. Inside. And out. I feel the slightest onset of some ancient, forgotten sensation or emotive state, like the dome of a mushroom pushing through tarmac. *Now, get to bed.*

HOODS

The job is a thing without end, something that will never come to fruition: it is incorporeal. It's something that is talked about, endlessly in the abstract, and has thus shucked off its form. Nevertheless, sometimes there can be practical stages on the road to nowhere.

Some of these stages are simple episodes of acquisition. There are tools and equipment required for this type of gambit. We all have our parts to play. Just as in the final act, throughout the preparation there are individual roles to perform.

Bill has a master list – I caught sight of it the other day for the first time as he was ticking something off. It runs to maybe a dozen sides of A4, I guess in some detail. The pages are somewhat dog-eared, as if Bill has worked through the info again and again into the small hours after Lauren and Justine have gone to bed, glugging back the malt and scratching his chin. He's not stupid, Bill, but he's also not the most imaginative sort of person. He's orthodox and methodical, practical at seeing the angles of what's in front of him. In some ways I envy him that: I'm the sort who is all imagination and no focus. I don't even think I exist in my immediate environment all the time, I'm off in a mental web of connections of things consonant with what I'm seeing, as if the whole thing is being played out on a screen. Bill is just where he is. It's the difference between denotation and connotation. Sometimes a lack of imagination is an asset. If all you can see is a vast litany of things that can go wrong, you might never even set out, which is why I'm not good at getting things started. You need someone like Bill for that. I just hope that he's covered enough of the angles to reduce our risk to the minimum. There are some things for which we can't legislate, for which we might have to improvise, so it's crucial that the basic parts are well rehearsed.

The day starts out early for me, as I have to pick up Mal before we head over to Edinburgh. Today I have the van, which is a shed compared to the Audi. It's slow, but it will do when it isn't too heavily loaded.

As soon as I see Mal's drawn, sour face I know I am in for a day of unconfined misery, cooped up in the van with him. These days I am beginning to feel like I deserve some level of punishment so, perversely, I eschew the M8 and take the slow route up the A71: Wishaw, Shotts, Addiewell, Bellsquarry.

I should really pay attention to the scenery like I used to, but nothing inspires me anymore. The world is a cold and damp place without reward. Its surface is hard beneath the patina of rain and I can't penetrate further into any meanings or mysteries. I may go places in the car, in the van, but they no longer take me to places in my head. Nothing changes there; I avoid myself as much as possible.

Mal's breath smells. He's been drinking and smoking and certainly hasn't cleaned his teeth. I'm guessing he's been wearing the same clothes for some days. I suspect flatulence. It's too cold to open a window. He pulls out a fag and lights up without asking, though it goes a little way to covering up the worst of the odours.

'Do you know where we're going?' I ask.

'Oh, aye.'

'I mean exactly.'

'I know where we're going, man, all right?'

'All right, I'll need directions: that's all.'

'No worries.'

He takes me on a route I could never retread if I tried. I think he's making it up as he's going along. It's like a walker's route: all turns. I'm sure I see the same junction twice from different angles. Mal lights a second Park Drive from the last and expectorates so long that it forces me to visualise what he's hawking up. I have had nought but coffee for breakfast, which is probably a blessing.

By and by we come to our destination, a trading estate consisting of a number of small cul-de-sacs of six-units-in-a-line: car tuners; double-glazing firms; a pet wholesalers. We're heading for a welding suppliers, one far away from our usual haunts. I pull up and Mal stubs out his cigarette, even though it is only half way down.

'Proper precautions,' he says.

The sign says 'No Naked Flames'. Gas bottles sit in

cages outside the premises. We enter through the shutter door and over to the trade counter. Mal knows what he wants.

I've never seen a plasma cutter before even if I've heard of them. We pay cash and manhandle the box into the back of the van. How much has Bill laid out on all of this already? You have to speculate to accumulate. We set off again.

'Just stop over there, John.'

It is breakfast time. We eat at a trailer parked at the entrance to the estate. Mal has two eggs in his bacon bap, which makes the top half slide all over the bottom and leak out bile-coloured yolk. Fuck knows what his digestion will make of all that on the way back – I'll take the M8 to speed things up. I opt for the lobster thermidor with wild rice and a nice Alsace Riesling just coming into its own. It looks like a sausage sandwich when it arrives.

Most of the situations in which you find yourself would mystify you if you'd been parachuted into them; it's only that you've come to them by an infinite series of subtle steps that you don't notice how far you've come. It's evolution by degrees and, suddenly, you find yourself perched on the tip of a substitute reality years or decades down the line from your starting point. It makes a mockery of choice. It's easy for the small changes to come about, for you to let them slip by unremarked, only to find that you've let yourself in for wholesale revolution when the picture finally forms.

Our next stop is an electrical suppliers for tape and the longest tie-wraps they have. Mal explains to the guy behind the counter that they're wanted for runs of power cable, so they need to be tough. I can tell when he's lying these days, because his voice takes on a more pally tone. He belches egg and Park Drive. 'I beg your pardon,' he says in faux aristocratic English, possible for my benefit.

Beg, you fucker; get it out before the drive back.

His tasks are over now and he's lost interest. With the extra driving around to break up our pattern of movement it's turned noon. I've got used to the run of the van. I have tasks. Thankfully, Mal wants to be dropped off at a boozer on the west side whilst I get on with my things. Once he's out of the van I am lighter and freer. The food might have something to do with it, more so that feeling that I always get when I'm alone on the road that, somehow reality can't get me if I keep on moving. The van rattles up the streets and I fish out the maps I've printed off the internet. I've been allowed up to the house for this task. I was even allowed to oust Lauren from the computer, where she was supposed to be revising (the browser history told more of a tale of social networking). She stayed in the room with me working through a volume on Media Studies, not one of my subjects. I could hear her breathing stop from time to time, as if halting to take on a new idea. I should have been concentrating more on my own work, but every time I'm near her I'm caught up too much in her field of radiation.

I pull over at a convenient point and compare my printouts with the A to Z. I am to buy masks for the occasion of our special night out. I could go to an Army and Navy and buy five black balaclavas, but that creates a conspicuous incident. So, first stop is the nearest bike shop.

I eye the bikes in the showroom. The market's moved on since I left my old sports bike out on the street in London. I'd love one of these new Ducatis: it's too long since I've been as free as that.

'Can I help you?'

'Yes, I need a thermal balaclava – could you show me what you've got?'

'Sure.' He looks disappointed not to be selling me something more substantial; maybe after the job.

'What are you riding now?' he says.

'Triumph Daytona, but I'm wondering about a change. Oh, and an old BMW R85 that doesn't go out much. I might get round to finishing it off eventually.' I lie well these days. Unlike Mal I don't have a different tone for untruths. Maybe I would if I ever rang true, but that never happens.

'You couldn't do better than that Duke: we sell a lot of them.'

I picture the queues of punters ranged round the block, cash ready for the next Ducati off the roll. For someone like me he would be better off playing the exclusivity card: 'Yes, we just keep the one in stock for the discerning buyer, blah, fucking blah...'

Still, they have a range of thermal balaclavas. I select one with individual eye and mouth holes rather than a single aperture, which wouldn't be much of a disguise.

'Tell you what, I'll have two – one for the wife – she says she feels the cold on the back.'

'Right.'

The next bike shop is miles away and it's a fucker to find. Driving around whilst navigating is never the easiest thing and far removed from the freedom of the open road, but I do find the place eventually and go through the same routine. Once more and I'll be done but, as luck has it, they have a sale bin with a loose balaclava in it, the holes outlined in contrasting tape. It looks like a pair of Y-fronts for an alien. I really hope Mal gets to wear this one, I really do. I can buy it legitimately as a supplemental bargain, which means I don't have to trawl around to the next shop on my list.

That's the end of my couture shopping trip. On the day we will all wear our own clothes as long as they are dark. There was some talk of matching boiler suits, but Bill vetoed that: fancy getting stopped by the Police five up in a panel van looking exactly like a gang. At least in our civvies, if we have to scatter we're not going to be too easy to spot. This is why it's all about the details and why, if you'd looked at your life twenty years ago there'd be no way of predicting you'd end up neck deep in this kind of shit.

It takes a long time to work my way back to Mal and I

have to go into the pub to pull him out. He's got comfortable and won't leave until he's had another one, which means he has to buy me one for justification. Then he wants to take his time. I know what's coming next. He's barely plonked the drinks on the table before he starts on about his divorce.

'She never understood what I'm about. See, I'm a sensitive man. I'm one of your poets. She just wanted me to go to work and provide the nice house and food and clothes for the wains and her fucking holidays in Tenerife.'

He emphasises the last 'e' to make it sound aspirational and pretentious. He's already thoroughly pissed and has reached the stage where he could nurse a pint for an hour. I would normally neck a first one in fifteen or twenty minutes. I'm driving. Sitting here and listening to Mal is like witnessing a man throw up in slow motion. The reason for your divorce, Mal, is that Mrs Mal couldn't bear to spend one more night in bed with you and all that might entail.

'...you see, that's my philosophy.'

I've missed some gem whilst attempting to block out unpleasant images. 'Drink up, Mal, or we'll keep Bill waiting.'

He's drunk just enough to become compliant. He blathers all the way through the return journey. I'm up to eighty on the motorway trying to cut down the time. I try to think of better things, but the only better thing I can think of is Lauren. Then I have to compare what she stands for with what I've become and that makes me sad, and sad for her in case she has to see, in her life, any if the things I've had to see, which leads me back to places I don't want to go and hence back to Mal to stop the pictures and so on, round in circles to Mal's fucking non-stop soundtrack and the cavernous booming of the knackered van.

As it happens we all wait on Bill back at the works. Euan and Deep have been shopping as well. We're all going to be doing a show-and-tell later for Bill's approval and, no doubt, for more ticks against the list.

'Bill phoned to say he's going to be some time,' says Deep.

Unfortunately, I know just what this means. Euan has increasingly been allowed to bring some of his stock into the empty warehouse. So now there are boxes of knock-off perfume and trainers on the shelves, as well as shrink-wrapped collections of porn DVDs. Euan's installed a player and TV in our office. He bangs on about this sort of stuff all the time: thirty-two inch this, forty-eight inch that, 1080 HD ready, plasma technology, to the point where I'd like to take Mal's plasma cutter to it all. Euan doesn't need much excuse to demonstrate his stock, so now we have to watch selections of favourite porn in giant screen format while we wait for the boss to turn up.

It would be fair to say that I'm something of an enthusiast for the naked female form, and I haven't got to my stage of life without seeing plenty of pornography, but there's nothing erotic about this stuff. There's too much 'Take it bitch' and 'Suck it whore' like there's a winner and loser at this game, all domination and enforced submission, no element of care or concern or empathy. The boys love it. They're all but joining in: 'See her, she's fuckin' into it', 'Go on woman, gag on that.' I have to watch, of course, otherwise I'd be gay and that can't be tolerated in this company, even in this century. Even though I'm driving I get hold of the whisky. Mal has moved on to the hard stuff and a whole new level of drunkenness. I'd rather be alone in the flat.

When Bill's not here the sub-hierarchy is much clearer. Euan's at the top. Mal thinks he's second, but he's at the bottom. Deep is interchangeable with me depending on what we're doing, unless I'm actually outside the system because of my alien origin.

Minutes have different textures depending on their context. Some slide smoothly past with barely a ruffle; rarely, some have transcendent qualities that will impact long after they have gone; others smoulder like old tyres, giving off acrid smoke that burns the eyes. There's a bad smell in the room right now, bitterness and alcohol.

'Look at this,' says Deep. He brings out a mobile phone, not too modern looking, maybe a little large by current standards.

'So? It's a phone,' says Euan.

'Ah yeah, but is it? Is it?' They're quite drunk now. 'That's what you're supposed to think.'

It's a phone, though it seems to have two stubby aerials.

'Now,' he says. He presses a button. Blue sparks crackle between the aerials. 'How about that? It's a stun gun. Looks just like a phone – you can't tell the difference. Millions of volts. Millions.'

He leans over to Mal and pushes the still sparking weapon towards his chest. 'Here, Mal, how about a little tickle, yeah?'

Mal tries to hold him off, 'Fuck off, man, fuck off.'

'Go on, tak yer medicine.'

'Fuck off you cunt, get it out my fuckin' face'

Euan's stood up now, egging him on. Coitus continues uninterrupted on the TV screen. 'Go on Deep, electrocute the wee twat.'

'Fuck off the both of you.'

Deep's getting very close to actual contact now. He has the smile of an idiot. Euan's getting ready to join in physically. Bill's at the door.

'Fuck it, settle down you lot. And turn that shit off. We've business to sort out.'

It's quiet quite quickly, though the choppy seas of Mal's torment take a while to settle. We report back to Bill on the outcome of our tasks. The job, the team, has a kind of structure, a mismatch of disparate parts that makes a form, a chimera. Bill is the head.

ART AND EXECUTION

It's late in the day. If I have any future at all, it consists of this job alone. Beyond that there is nothing. I am subsumed solely into this task. I am the task. I am engineered for it and, when it is done, I will cease to function. That's why I don't think too far ahead. I could see how a lack of ambition might be liberating in other circumstances, but not when you are fissured with self contempt.

The exhibition has commenced: Art and Execution. It runs for two weeks. One way or another, we will have to have executed our plan within a fortnight. All the preparation builds to just one night, one crux of activity. Like the best building work, it's all in the preparation. We have been inside the exhibition hall twice – once legitimately and once not; now we have to repeat the cycle. Only myself, Bill and Mal will go. Euan and Deep have nothing to add: they have better things to do elsewhere.

Today has an odd stillness about it. The drizzle has stopped for once and the sky brightened oppressively behind its unbroken cap of cloud. I feel like I need sunglasses or a wide-brimmed hat, even though it's still just the middle of March. I park the Audi in a multi-storey half a mile away from the hall and we leave independently, Mal first – he doesn't do patience. Me next, after half an hour in a bar set up like someone's lounge. People go about their business. I am a criminal. I'm dressed in black like a villain. I should have shades and an entourage, at least a moll ready with a fag lighter. I don't smoke. There are a couple of girls with big glasses of wine at lunch time. It's a week day. The girls are maybe representatives, one in a pin-striped suit and the other in a sharp skirt and jacket. The skirted one has cream tights or stockings and flat shoes she could drive in. They're near me but slightly higher up, on a raised area. I'm at a table by the window, facing into the bar. I can see their legs below the table at which they're sitting. They're talking, but I can't hear what they're saying over the background noise. That's the trouble with all these hard surfaces: they don't dampen the echoes.

I can look without appearing to stare by facing slightly past them and shifting my gaze back towards them. I can quickly look away and pretend I was looking at a distant thought. Their mouths make shapes with the words, carmine red and black cherry.

My old leather jacket creaks. It's been rained on too many times. In some places its blackness has worn through to a grey brown like dusty spider webs. I have so few possessions now I know each one of them intimately. Who knows these women that well? Time to go.

***

The hall is very busy. I've been seeing the posters around town for weeks and I reckon the organisers are keen for good returns. Thinking of all the preparation they've put in: the initial concept, finance, feasibility analysis, transport, brochure copy, print lead times, tickets, proofs, photos, discussion, re-discussion, deliveries, acres of paperwork, overtime, burning the midnight oil, the logistics of tearing down the last exhibition, clearing out and setting up the next.

And we've followed our own phantom course: an idea, planning, access, personnel, best practice, our opening night, only we have much less paperwork and more limited access to resources.

I don't feel too self-conscious this time. Mooching around with my paid-up ticket is a far cry from padding around like a ghost recording footage those few long weeks ago. I don't think we should even have bothered coming separately: with all these people we could never be singled out as anything.

The space is much different to how it was set up for the computer fair. Now there are zones set out in themes. The first I come to is *Ceramics*, more likely ceramic sculpture, I think. There are cabinets containing selections of glazed and unglazed artefacts, some obviously jugs, bowls and plates, others more abstract. It's all quite calming, like a provincial museum.

Next to this is a section on steelwork, figures and

forms constructed from car parts and scrap, a face from the crown-wheel of a differential, valve fingers mushrooming to flat ends. I guess I'm supposed to see a human skeleton, but my petrol-head mind can't stop trying to identify the constituent parts. I look into the dead face for a moment, before moving my attention to a Wellington chest seemingly cobbed together form washing-machine shells. It's all very well in a wouldn't-give-it-houseroom kind of way. We are informed further by a layout of the sculptor's kit, gas tanks, goggles and assorted torches, bringing me back to my afternoon with Bill and Mal working steel for our project.

Steel moves on to wood in the form of bespoke furniture, in hues of pale oak and cherry, maple and beech, beautifully shaped and put together, sometimes with hints of bark incorporated into the designs. The pieces are priced at apoplexy-inducing levels. For the first time I think about the prospect of making some money out of all of this. It's too long since I've felt the quality of real wads of folding. Without it I can't really do a proper job of being my pretend self. Money lubricates in every way; lack of it leads to desiccation and decay. Money makes the merry-go-round – the spalted ash wardrobe is six thousand eight hundred pounds.

By turns I reach the main draw: an ongoing performance of live jewellery making, centre stage with cabinet after cabinet of hand-crafted earrings, necklaces, brooches and tiaras, along with nose studs, belly piercings and conspicuous bling-sized chunks of gold.

It's set out as a jewellery workshop with long benches. There are four jewellers: an older guy, two younger ones and a woman in her early thirties. She has the relaxed look of someone who has always worked in the arts. She's putting together something that looks like a salamander on a leaf. You can watch from behind a velvet rope. She is used to being watched even though the exhibition has only been running for a few days. I am allowed to watch, her fingers playing a fine file back and forth across the silver like a violin bow, the only music a low rasp. The tip of her tongue reaches out to her top lip as she concentrates on the exactness of it all. I'm not sure who's concentrating most, she on the work or me on the worker. I look from above, the line of her nose, the way her eyebrows delineate her brow, the way her dark hair parts at the crown and falls to her shoulder, her forearms resting lightly on the bench. The salamander is a fleet form in her hands, a small fish twisting in a pool, flashing the silver of its underside in the sunlight.

'Leave it you fucker.'

Mal passes just behind, speaking under his breath purely for my benefit. I'm supposed to be on a job, so I take the advice and move on.

The layout of the building is familiar to me now. We've been through the camera footage a number of times. I know what's behind each door, which are offices, which are stairs, I have a fair idea of where I am in relation to the floor beneath in all its dowdy, behind-the-scenes glory. Already I am projecting lines of movement onto the current layout, how we might proceed once we are inside. God, that could be tonight if Bill said so, though there's not much chance of that. There's still too much to do before we're properly ready. I'm not sure I'll ever be ready, but that's not going to influence Bill. I see him by the jewellery exhibit looking longingly into one of the cabinets. Mal is unseen in the increasing crowd.

I look at my watch. I'm all but done here. The rest of the exhibition is to do with the technology of production. I pass the printing and DVD production stands by the left wall. There are fewer people here. The information is on standing boards, with displays of fabulous printing effects and, further on, all the stages of DVD mastering and manufacture. The displayed machines look like giant photocopiers.

I guess Mal is off checking our access route in the stairwell once again. That was one of his jobs. I might wander off back to the car and think about what I've seen, try not to think too much about dark-haired lady jewellers and try to understand how we're possibly going to manage to pull this off.

'Did you see the security on all those gems though?' Mal's only been in the car three seconds, 'Pressure pads, volumetric, the whole fucking nine yards, whoa!'

'What about the window?' Bill.

'It was locked again, but there's nothing different

there. Someone will just have to go in during the day and unlock it – piece of piss.'

'You'll do that.'

'Oh aye, I'll do that all right,'

We're still in the car park. Bill even has brochures from the exhibits, like a regular punter. Mal has a post card of one of the metal sculptures. 'See? I could do that – there's fucking nothing to it. The worst bit's having to use a barrier between the ferrous and the ally. Bob's your uncle – three thousand quid please.'

I doubt whether Mal has the artistic temperament, though doubtless he has the skills. All drunks reduce things to the simplistic, even those expostulating great themes at the expense of a quiet evening in the pub.

Bill's quiet again. I think it's gone well. There were a few extra security bods compared to the computer fair, but I'm thinking that the expense will limit their numbers during the night. This is one of those areas where we are just going to have to see. We know they have lots of electronic security: that might make them underplay the personnel. Risk assessment by accountants.

'All right,' says Bill, 'we'll get off. We look like a bunch of gangsters hanging round here. If I did it again we'd go in suits.'

'I don't have a suit Bill.'

'Fuck it, Mal, what about your wedding suit?'

'I'll never get in that – the trousers are a twenty-eight.'

Fifteen inches too few, I reckon, but I haven't got a suit myself. My criminal wages don't cover a suit of the sort of quality I like: I'll have to get on to the union.

I press the pedals and drive off. There will be more meetings, but not so many now before the job. Even though it's just Bill and a few guys going about business, there's a real presence to it. The job has a life of its own, breathing hot steam from its nostrils and champing at the bit. Once released from its chains there's no going back. The die is cast, I've thrown in my lot and every fucking cliché you can think of. One day you're a spectator, the next you're embroiled in highly illegal money-making schemes. I place my paid token in the machine at the barrier and we leave the car park. I drive out of town. Beyond the precincts of Scottish suburbia we come across a slow-moving hatchback. I gun the Audi and leave him behind. 'Fuck me,' says Mal. Bill sits quietly in the passenger seat staring straight ahead. I'm up to ninety and rapidly catching up with another slow mover. 'Have him,' says Bill, so I knock it down one and fire past, free for a moment from the world of pain.

GIRLS

After the visit to the exhibition I have another few days on my own, but I can stand it as Bill has a trip lined up for me.

I take the Audi and Lauren and we collect Yvonne from her house. Yvonne's mum gives me one of her looks, even though I've dressed as well as I can for the occasion. We are shopping in Glasgow. It's Saturday and it takes a long time to get through the heavy traffic. Shopping means clothes shopping. I don't know any of the clothes shops. When I think about it I don't suppose I've been in a ladies' boutique for twenty years, but apparently Lauren and Yvonne know every outlet in Glasgow intimately. They also have a well-rehearsed route to cover them all in the least possible time. The same goes for their pattern of behaviour in each store: it's assessed for stock viability, range and sizes style potential, all in a matter of seconds, and then allocated proportionate time to do it justice. None of the consideration is tacit, but proceeds in a torrent of 'What are they thinkings' and 'Look, Lauren, it's just like Keira's in *Heat*'.

I'm stunned. I suppose it's prejudice, but I'd never thought of teenage girls as systematic. Yet here they are, tearing through an entire shop in just a few minutes making value judgements at a microcosmic level on every item in nine hundred foot square premises, and then onto the next until...

They find something they like. Time slows down like a stone dropped in treacle. Items are pawed over and examined and held against others to check for matches. Now it's 'Whad'ya think, Yvonne, whad'ya think?' and 'How many can we take in the changing rooms?'

I am a sore-thumb geezer in a world of girls. Pairing my smart jacket with my jeans and dark blue shirt has made me look like someone trying to sell something. Even though it's cold March everyone else is in summer gear: thin tops, bare midriffs, wide plastic belts that I remember from the last time, now part of social history, big jewellery, big accessories, wide-mouthed shoulder bags full of everything. Everyone has straight hair regardless of how it started out. No one, but no one, is above half my age, staff or otherwise. I pick the darkest backgrounds to hide against, but the pallid moon of my face gives me away. I stand; girls pass by freshly minted in Boots No. 7, hair managed to the micron.

Lauren has found a dress to try on and, for some reason she has decided to show it to me. 'What do you think, John?'

It is pale and floral, almost an archetypal granny dress as far as I'm concerned, but a wee bit shorter. Her shoulders are smooth and connect seamlessly to her neck. For god's sake don't give me a twirl, but she does, leaves no time for comment (a small blessing) and sweeps back to Yvonne, who has appeared outside the changing rooms in micro shorts and nought but an elastic band encircling her bosom between midriff and décolletage. I think I hear something like, 'Do I dare, Lauren, do I dare?' before they disappear upstage to leave me wondering about drinks in the interval.

She will buy the dress. The price would get me a passable suit. Yvonne has eschewed the elastic but has found what I might call the top half of a cardigan. I would be a gentleman and offer to carry their bags, but I know they won't let me. I stand a way off while they disburse their credit cards and chatter, chatter. A sales child notices me waiting and says, 'Come shopping with your daughter? That's nice. You don't see that too often.' And, rather than appear to be a dirty old man, I say, 'Yes, I thought it would be nice to spend time with the girls.' Hoping she won't detect that we have completely different accents.

The cold air strikes my lungs. The girls lead me on. The shop girl had given me a slight look of sympathy, as if the whole expedition might be a chore, but what else would I be doing? Sitting in my cold flat on my own? Staring at the limitless sky?

We carry on through a couple more places. The girls are happy. Without a word they step into a cafe bar.

How is it when those things which are most normal feel the most strange? I sit with my cappuccino in the company of everyday people doing everyday things, but I am far from everyday. I feel like something subhuman or unreal or improperly formed. I've lost those things that make it possible to feel comfortable or fully engaged even in the most mundane situations. It's to do with the things I've seen, I'm sure, but also what I've become. It could never have been predicted. To look at me from the outside I could be a normal guy spending time out with the girls, sipping a normal cup of coffee in a normal way, but on the inside I'm this apparition struggling with the pretence.

The girls are too busy speaking to each other to speak to me. I don't mind. I watch the movements of Lauren's mouth as she speaks even if I don't hear all of the words. My ciabatta arrives. The girls are having cakes. I've paid: it's inconceivable that it should be another way even though the bill smarted. I crunch through the bread to find the mozzarella unmelted within. In stark contradiction, a whole cherry tomato has become superheated and explodes white hot pulp onto my tongue. I try not to show it. A woman at an adjacent table orders a 'focaccia bread', which makes me want to launch into a diatribe on tautologies, but my mouth-parts are scalded.

It is possible to be half somewhere and half somewhere else. That must be the case if you are only half there. For me that is permanently the case. Perhaps it's so that you can't fully register the full experience of your own disappointments. Even at my best I fail to scale the dizzy heights of mediocrity. I stop myself: I'm out with the girls. Even if I can no longer be properly human, this is the best that it gets for me. On the odd occasions that I have company, it's invariably with men. Taking Lauren to school is a treat, but this is proper social interaction.

I watch them talking, the shapes made by their lips, their clear eyes. Even the slight darkness beneath Lauren's eyes is fleeting evidence of one too many late nights and no sign of the passage of hard years. I wonder how I look when I am like this, kind of vacant with faint ghosts of anxiety crossing my face.

Yvonne has one of her purchases half out of its bag and is demonstrating some salient feature to Lauren. They are talking in low tones, so I can't hear, but I've heard my name and am coming back to find what it's about. They look at me as if I've only just appeared.

'So, you won't tell Dad, John, will you?'

'Uh?'

'About the party.'

'What party?'

'I knew he hadn't heard, Lauren, he's daydreaming.'

But I have heard, because you can take things in without consciously paying attention. 'You mean the party on Friday when you're both supposed to be doing revision round at Kirsty's? That party?'

'Don't tell Dad, will you?'

'What? That you've told him that you're all convening at Kirsty's next Friday for an all-evening review of your coursework when, actually, you two are taking a cab over to Glasgow to a do at some boy's house?'

This is my little bit of power. They look concerned. I imagine that the boy or boys who will be at the party are worth the subterfuge, even if the function itself is apparently beyond parental approval. These are small lies. I wish mine were thus.

I let them dangle for a moment. Obviously, I'm not going to scupper their plans, but I allow myself the small satisfaction of letting the moment linger. 'I won't tell him. He doesn't have to know everything.'

With that they're straight back into their conversation, discussing when the cab's going to collect them and in which order; I'm back to myself and my burnt mouth. I try not to imagine Yvonne in the semi-transparent thing she is showing to Lauren: in this company I might as well be eighty.

BRAINCELLS

You would think that preparations for the job would take place behind locked doors under conditions of strictest secrecy, but most of it seems to involve getting out and seeking stuff. Some of this stuff is merely information.

One of the things we need is a false registration number for the works van. It needs to be a number from an exact equivalent, a van of the same model, colour and age. This would seem to be straightforward enough for a common or garden white Luton, but that's not so. Twice I have been stationed in a café next to a busy road, notebook at the ready, sipping coffees for three hours at a stretch, nibbling at the odd pastry, cursing each time I have to use the toilet because I know that at exactly that moment a suitable candidate is dribbling past. Plenty of vans go by; many of them are white; none of them are remotely the right age. That's the problem: the works van is excessively superannuated – any company with decent cash flow would have replaced it with a newer model years ago.

Without results, Bill has decided we have to take an active approach. Apparently, he's been keeping his eye out for weeks. After I've dropped Lauren off at school I call back at the house and park up next to Euan's new

BMW coupe. For the first time I notice that it's a similar shade of silver to Bill's Audi. I go straight in – Bill doesn't want to be bothered answering the door – and find them sitting in the living room. I have a slight sense that I've walked in on something, but I don't know what: I haven't really seen Bill and Euan together before without anyone else present.

'I've left the keys on the hall stand.' I say.

'Good, we're done here.'

I get myself comfortable in the black leather passenger seat of the BM. Euan is driving. I don't like being a passenger – I'm a driver. I'm not too enamoured with his choice of music, either. I don't even know what it is, some kind of composition consisting purely of beat and thumping, unmelodic bass. But it's an ideal soundtrack for Euan, as he's taken Bill's advice to cover plenty of ground literally and is blasting around the lanes in a frenzy.

The only peace I've had in my recent life has been alone at the wheel, so putting up with Euan is doubly difficult. He's just not very good at driving fast. He's not smooth, he's on and off the brakes, accelerating to a halt, failing to anticipate problems and dealing with them in a panic when he gets to them. I'm supposed to be spending my time looking out for vans, but instead I'm braking by proxy and trying not to shout out loud when he's missed an obvious hazard. All this to the dreadful 'thumpa-thumpa' beat with its sudden and unpredictable breaks into full-on cacophony. Euan is not much younger than me, but he's from a completely different generation with totally different tastes.

One of his problems is that he leans forward in his seat, meaning that all his attention is concentrated ahead, on a small portion of road maybe thirty yards away and, therefore, nowhere else, not in the mirrors or to the side or even close to, where there may be stones in the road or parts dropped off motor vehicles. In just half an hour we have run over two hard objects: God knows what the tyres cost on this thing.

There are too many facets to this job, too many men engaged in too many variables. It's getting hard to see it all coming together. All these weeks have been about maybe an hour's activity when it comes down to it. That hour has to go right, or we're all in the shit. So what's this undisciplined shooting about going to achieve?

We fuck about going to Eaglesham and down the A77 to Kilmarnock. It's not a bad gambit in theory, as there may well be vans plying their trade down the dual carriageway. Euan does seventy, then he does a hundred, then he tailgates vehicles in the outside lane. My attention wanders to the scenery, but I don't care about it. Elsewhere in the world there are ancient white Luton vans studiously being somewhere else, in far flung counties, just over the next mountain, in a road tunnel directly under us as we pass over at a hundred and ten, apparently.

I look everywhere, even over to the opposite

carriageway, which is a complete waste of time as I have no chance of catching a number at this speed even if the barrier on the central reservation wasn't in the way.

At last, Euan's CD comes to an end; unfortunately, it's on continuous replay. I reach for the eject button.

'What are you doing?'

'Thought we'd have a change.'

'Leave it.'

I don't think Euan wants to be doing this. I think that he'd rather it was someone else. Perhaps that's why he's driving so quickly, because the time will go quicker. I haven't had anything to eat for breakfast, again. I've just had two coffees, which are beginning to wear off. Kilmarnock to Irvine and now the roads are busy. Euan's bottled up in traffic and I'm bottled up in the car with him. I'm not used to being with people anymore. I feel their presence too keenly when I actually have to spend time with them. Bill is easy. He doesn't radiate too far unless he's about something important. Euan is all radiation – his energy spills over into you all the time and upsets your status quo. I look at the car stereo to see if the repeat function is optional, but nothing is obvious there. We spin on. So does the CD.

By the end of the third run-through of thumpa-thumpa I have lost track of where I am. It's one of those disorientation tortures where no rest is permitted, the prisoner is intimidated with ear-splitting sounds and spun round and round until he loses all sense of direction. The only human contact the prisoner is allowed is with his captors. I decide not to be a victim and break the ice.

'Where are we, Euan?'

'Fuck knows, I've never been out here before.'

I can believe that. All the boys are so much part of their place compared to myself that I can see them being out of place very easily. We've ended up on a network of minor roads and Euan just doesn't sit right.

'Tell you what, why don't we head back towards Glasgow? There's fuck all traffic here, the chances of seeing the right sort of van are next to nil.'

He thinks for a moment, ' All right, which way?'

'I'll have to have a look at the map.'

'What map?'

'Don't you have a map?'

'No.'

Great, I shall now navigate by the stars, except that the only one that's out is the big one and it's hidden behind its honour guard of grey cloud. I guess which is east: if we keep heading east we will hit some road that will take us back to the city.

I don't really know any of these boys in any real sense. They don't do friendship as I might imagine it. But they're not well contained. Unlike me they give themselves away all the time. Euan hates being told what to do. It doesn't feature in his personal image of himself. But I don't think he's got the gumption on all fronts. Thumpa-thumpa has restarted and has got to the bit where it degenerates into drums only for an indeterminate number of interminable minutes. I reach over and press the eject button. The CD pops out like a silver tongue.

'What the fuck?'

'That's enough of that Euan, I can't hear myself fucking think.'

'Put it back.'

I look directly across at him. I know he can see me a bit, even though he's focused on his tiny spot of road. 'No.' I say pull the CD out of its slot and put it away in the glove box. There's no case for it. Euan says nothing. 'Try a left up here,' I say.

He takes the left and, as luck would have it, or all my years of experience in delivery and despatch, we hit the A737 heading towards Paisley and Glasgow. Even when I'm not driving, I'm in charge when it comes to vehicles.

We have worn through to the afternoon and I need a piss, quite badly. We haven't stopped once and I wouldn't mind something to eat. Euan eats a lot of food for his body building but I've also observed that he doesn't feel the compulsion to eat like I do; we're made of different stuff. There has been an end to conversation since the incident with the van. I saw it briefly on the other side of the dual carriageway on the M8 past Govan. This resulted in a hectic sequence of sprinting up the road, overtaking on the wrong side, diving off the next available exit, struggling to get back on the opposite side in the face of countless dawdlers, redlining it to try and catch up and then finding the van had left into dense traffic. The following half hour saw us attempting to queue hop in an urban area, Euan's point-and-squirt technique adding to the discomfort of my own desire to point and squirt, my driver's overbearing competitive spirit really kicking in with a vengeance.

The van was our Moby Dick, seen at a distance as an impossible quarry, never stationary for long enough to get out and run up to, Euan desperate to get it over with, taking stupid risks finally getting close, getting the number, getting past and away and…

'I hate to tell you this.'

'What?'

'It won't do.'

'What do you mean?'

'It won't do, it's too new.'

'No way. It's exactly the fucking same. It's exactly the same as Bill's van.'

'It's not. The cab's different – a newer model.'

'Fuck you, that'll do for us.'

'It might do for us, but will it do for Bill?'

He needed some more thinking time for this: a couple of minutes, but there can be only one conclusion when it comes to doing stuff for Bill.

'Shit, shit, shit,' he said and thumped the wheel.

It's been silence ever since and I'm even missing thumpa-thumpa a bit. I haven't even been offering directions. It's familiar territory for Euan anyway. His pumped-up physique has deflated a little in his seat. He's even driving slower. We're limping down the A74, which is just as well, as the fuel warning beeper went off some time ago. I've had enough of this myself, so when we pull into Bothwell Services I tell Euan I'm going to the main service area to get myself a sandwich from the shop. I don't give him time to say 'no'. Perhaps he's keen to see the back of me for a few minutes while he fills up.

It hits me while I'm waiting in line to pay for my grub.

'We're doing this all wrong,' I tell Euan when I get back to the car.

'What are you talking about?'

'We're chasing after vans. Where do you find vans and lorries?'

'Tell me.'

'In their designated parking areas at motorway service stations.'

There isn't a suitable van at Bothwell or Abington, which is as far as either of us want to go: it feels a little like leaving and I have no business anywhere else. But there is one at Harthill when we head out on the M8. It's a filthy fucking Luton of exactly the right age and looks likes it's been sitting and waiting for us for days, laughing its socks off. I get its number before it escapes.

'You fucking beauty,' says Euan. It's the nicest thing he's ever said to me.

I have to wait a long time in the workshop that Euan takes me to next. It's one of those back-street garages that reminds me of the place that I used to inhabit when I first pitched up with Terence and Dave prior to the inception of The Route. The place smells of pear drops. It's the paint. There's an old Rolls in here, a Silver Shadow, being resprayed. As I've got time to kill I take a closer look. The old Connolly hides that once graced the seats have been removed and replaced with bright pink leatherette studded with innumerable diamante crystals. I try not to heave. It's an old Shadow, as well, early Seventies, a grand old lady, come to this.

Other than that, there isn't much sign of work going on. Euan disappeared with some old mate as soon as we arrived, taking the number plate information with him. With the new rules it's really difficult to get new plates made up, precisely to obviate what we're doing here: getting false plates made up for the van.

After I'd been waiting half an hour I went for a wander down the unlit corridor that had swallowed up Euan and his mate, only to be turned back by a group of guys playing cards in a side room with a 'Where the fuck are you going?' Oh, yes, just like old times. since then it's just been me and my Shadow, gradually getting high on paint fumes and wondering whether I'll be eating more than a sandwich this fine day.

It's an hour before Euan comes back with the plates. I remember his anecdote about off-loading those stolen luxury cars and guess he's done this sort of thing before.

Since we got that number he's been as pleased as punch and he's evidently had a good old time chewing the fat with his old mucker, because the plates couldn't have taken more than a few minutes to make. Anyway, what would be the point of complaining about the wait? It's not that I have anything better to do, just that I'm hungry and I could do with getting home and getting something proper to eat.

Sadly, it's not to be, because Euan has some of his own business. It's already mid evening and dark. Even in town the overcast darkness is barely held back by the street lights, as if the ancient forces of nature are set to engulf the fragile veneer of civilisation if only there was a power cut. I'm the only person that feels this. Euan doesn't give a toss.

'I've got to go to the club,' he says, and we screech off once more through the congested network of towns.

It's Starz club, where Euan and Deep do some of their door work and some measure of their dealing. Euan walks up to the duty doorman like he owns the place.

'Carlo, this is John. He's with me.'

We bypass the queue and go straight inside. It's busy even at this early hour, which puzzles me until I notice the 'Two shots for One Happy Hour' posters.

'I've got to see the boss for a bit. Make yourself at home. I could be some time.'

Surely not, Euan, just take your time and don't bother about me. Get yourself a three course meal while you're about it. I'll stand here and slowly dissolve from the inside.

I gather from the bar man that two shots for one means precisely that and not half price for a single. I sit at the bar with my two whiskies thinking about dinner right up until the point where a young woman in purple court shoes walks past. The light catches glitter in her black top. Her friend is wearing a very short skirt and what appears to be a dog collar. Suddenly my hunger pangs go on the back burner. My tastes wouldn't normally run to dolled-up girls like these but I have been on my own a very long time.

I know that Euan is going to keep me waiting again. Everything's a performance with him, as if film cameras are recording his every move and he needs to look cool at all times. He's the star of the show and I'm just a supporting act. He's right at home here, where all the clientele are dressed to impress, the boys with their artfully untucked shirts, gold chains, bling rings and flash watches; the girls in their crop tops, micro skirts and straight-as-a-die haircuts. I must look like a down and out in my perished leather jacket and work strides. I feel down, and I've been out of it for ever. I get two more whiskies to bolster my spirit.

It's only later, when I'm feeling a bit wobbly and on my way to the bogs that I realise that we have, in fact, wasted the whole fucking day and all we needed to do was to go on to any auction website and search for a van for sale similar to ours and nick its number. When did I become so stupid? Whenever it was it has become permanent, as I leave the gents on the wrong tack and end up entering some stock room, where Euan is deep in conversation with someone, deep enough, luckily, not to notice my mistake before I can slip back out the door. I decide to punish my stupid crew of stupid brain cells by killing some of them by way of setting an example to the others with whatever brand of proprietary ethanol is still available at a two-for-one.

DRESSING

The morning wears on in its own way with nothing to do. Same too the afternoon. Eventually I give in and start on the bars. I have reached a threshold. I can get about four fifths of the way if I warm up right. Then I'm scuppered. I've tried to get further, but my will gives out. Even within each attempt there are barriers to cross, but I have a technique to allow for rest without breaking the rules.

It's cold where they keep the cars, but I am soon warm and then hot, rising and falling with the structure of the roof. At those points where it's too hard to go on, I wrap my arms and legs around one of the horizontals and rest like a sloth until I can build up the momentum to go on. My heart pounds in the silence and I wonder how much better I would have been at this at twenty rather than forty. When I am hugged close to the bar I can almost fall asleep. It's not much of an effort compared to hanging by one's arms, but it emphasises the solitude, which then compels you to go on. All things are like this: you may not come to rest because it reminds you that you will once stop and never go again.

'John?'

It is Lauren, standing inside the garage door. I have

never known her come to the garage before. I uncoil from the bar and drop on to the concrete floor. My feet make a smacking sound that echoes off the garage walls. I am sweating a lot. She looks at me oddly. Of course, I am wearing nothing but my track suit trousers.

'Hi,' I say, as if I am someone cool. Sweat runs into my eye and stings. I squint. It's suddenly quite awkward and there's a gap. We both speak at the same time.

'Dad says...'

'What can I do for you?'

'... could you come up to the house?'

More pause, 'Do I have time to get cleaned up?'

'I don't think so, he seemed to want you straight away.'

I expect her to leave now that she's delivered her news, so when she doesn't the awkwardness raises its ugly head again. I stand sweating in the half light of the garage trying to catch my breath whilst she looks directly at me with no tells on her face. For a brief moment I recall some shadow of a feeling from the time before this afterlife. I can't register it properly in its umbral form, but it has a notion of something important. That's as much as I can feel. A question forms, one of those slight seconds in which someone is set to speak, but it never happens. The moment goes and the question hangs. I look at her and she waits. I see her waiting. Of course, she hasn't been merely sent to tell me, I'm to follow her back to the house.

'I'll get a shirt.' It answers nothing.

***

Turns out that Bill just wants to go through the footage again. He needn't bother: I can go through it in my sleep, even though it's not me I detect as the source of the images. When you live in the very moment, anything that you have done that was weeks ago was done by someone else.

We're watching on the small set in the study, because Justine is home. The sound is turned down low. After all, we are engaged in a conspiracy.

'Like a drink, John?'

'Just water, thanks.'

He pours me a glass from a jug that he's using to water his whisky. I'm just too hot to drink the hard stuff right now. I probably smell.

He sounds out the stages and we go though the familiar route, 'Stair well...main hall, quickly...office next door...next room...'

I've heard it all before. I've got it. Bill sounds it out like something he's seen on a film. The footage has been edited now, so that it follows the steps that I will have to take on the evening. That's because I'm the one that's supposed to go in first. Still, I drift off.

'What?'

'Here John, you see?'

'I want you to look at this.'

He freezes the frame and someone that was me stops 'Here!'

still and holds their breath.

'What is it?'

'It's that camera. It sees you.'

'Does it?'

'You don't think it does, but it does.'

'It wasn't on, though, was it?'

'But it will be on, on the night.'

We've been building up to this for too long. It will never now happen. There have been too many preparations and there are too many things to go wrong. Because of all the questions it cannot be entirely resolved. Bill makes his points, I respond with platitudes. We discuss the nature of cameras and whether someone will register your presence if it's just a split second in the corner of a screen they're not really watching. It is simply the reading of a script for a play that will never be staged. Still, we carry on for an hour, then half an hour until Bill's said what he wants and I am free to go back to my flat.

'Mind if I use the phone?'

'Go ahead.'

I go though to hall telephone and reel through the yellow pages until I find some place to eat that sounds right and isn't too far without being near. I make a call, then one for a taxi. When I look up Lauren is standing at the bottom of the stairs. She's making this a habit.

'What do you think?'

She has on the dress she bought the other day, the one that's for the party. She has accessorised it with a wide belt. Her face is different. More made up.

What do I think? Too many things for comfort. 'Charming.'

'Is that all?'

'Sorry, thought that was enough.'

'Charming is what granddad used to say when he thought I'd said something rude.'

'Okay, you remind me of Paula Wilcox when she was in her prime.'

'Who's that?'

I have just realised that I am impossibly old, far too old to have any meaning in Lauren's presence. Her nails are painted in a dark shade, the first time I've seen them painted at all. She is barefoot regardless of her level of preparation from there on up.

'It must be an important party.'

'What do you mean?'

'It's got to be an important party if you need a dress rehearsal.'

'Does it?'

'Yeah, I guess, doesn't it?'

'No. That's what's good about clothes: you can enjoy them even when you're just trying them on.'

'I still can't help thinking that there must be someone special coming to justify all this preparation.'

For the first ever that I have seen, she blushes and seems incapable of a reply. I don't care to see her feeling awkward. 'Paula Wilcox: it's a compliment. She was very beautiful. Still is, actually.'

She softens and smiles, ‘You like the outfit, then?’
‘Of course, it’s perfect.’

BARS

Everyone has someone. Bill has Justine and Lauren, Euan has Debbie, Deep at the very least has his sister Prema, even Mal has his ex-wife in some sense. I have no one. There is no job, so there is nothing left for me but the continued narrowing down of options and arteries.

It's on my own at night that I feel the loneliness most. You would think that, with so little of me left, I would no longer have the facility or desire to make a connection, but something at the very base of me craves an echo in the silence.

I feel it in the early hours during episodes of insomnia and in the long evenings during the preparation of my solitary meals and their aftermath. All my past except for the images that haunt me so much, has fallen away as I've climbed to my remote pinnacle in a black windswept void, looking out forever into the infinite dark whilst the wind stings my face and salt water runs from the corners of my eyes.

Tonight I have picked up Lauren from school and taken her over to Yvonne's. I have brought the car back to the garage where it has cooled in that clicking way that cars do. Now I am drinking. I have two bottles of

Australian Shiraz on a two-for-the-price-of-one-and-a-half offer. The number of alcoholic units is displayed on the back label, but there is no level-of-maudlin warning. I'm drinking so fast that there isn't enough time for the alcohol to register properly in my system. This usually only happens when I drink spirits, which is always a precursor to falling straight into bed and passing out. It's far too early to do that. I try to slow down. Sometimes, I wonder why I don't cry, but perhaps the deaths of both of my parents in quick succession all that time ago put paid to that. Tears don't solve anything.

I've decided that avoiding the past doesn't work. It's okay for not reliving all the mistakes and re-running the film scenes of your misdemeanours, but it doesn't stop the effect. You may not remember it all, but the sum total of all the shit and strife comes up unbidden. You are your past and you feel the weight of it. Tar seeps through the surface of the road and sticks to you.

For a while I sit with the lights off and stare out of the window. There are no other houses close by. There is no one outside; there is no one else inside the garage. I stare into the bedroom. Who lived here? Some handyman/chauffeur? *Plus ça change?*

There is nothing to see inside or out except an eternity of night and, yet, this is Bill's paradise. It's all to do with who you're with, though I guess the nice house helps.

The glass in my hand is empty. I am well in to the second bottle. Swigging directly from the bottle would save time, but it's one step too far. I'm imagining prowlers. This time it's not kids casing the joint for valuables, but sprites and spirits filtering up from their rock beds through the wet pasture beyond the garden. They gain substance as they react with the air, so long time since the last time. They're shuffling slowly, inexorably, drawn by the light of Bill's house, a beacon in the black landscape. The sheep in the field twitch and pull away as black eyes settle on the prize of light. They enter through the fence. They've been here for millennia, biding the while in their tombs in the strata, sucking time through clenched teeth and waiting to wake again. And sometimes, when the waiting and sleeping become too much, they float slowly to the surface in search of life, to feed on the warm glow of its presence, to see what's changed since the last time, to dream of how they were once themselves when they lived, in the forests of yew and juniper and the jumping hare, amongst the outcropped rocks and running rivulets of spring when the world moved to the music of harmony in the concert of natural events.

I take my hard chair to the bedroom window to get a better view of the house. It's near, but far enough. Keep the staff at arm's length. Maybe there was a cook/housekeeper married to the chauffeur. They both lived here, when the paint was fresh and it was a real step up from the old tenement flat. I swill the wine around my mouth before I swallow it. Where's my companion and helpmeet? Nothing comes back. I grow cold as midnight comes and goes, watching sprites and demons lingering in the shadows between the firs, half-formed in light motes, sometimes there, sometimes not, the brain making sense out of the blackness. I pour out the last glass and make a play of wringing out the bottle even though there is only me to enjoy the joke.

I am impossibly weary. There is nothing else to drink. I could sleep forever, but the chattering noise in my head will stop me even getting started. I know this feeling well. For years the future has signified nothing. I've rubbed along badly. I've used up my existence and squandered it on fuck all. I haven't even gambled it. If I'd have gambled it, at least there would have been a chance of winning something. We're all born with a little in the pot. Mine went on booze and binges and meaningless displays of wealth like the worst lottery winners. Now my thin-spun thread of life has stretched out to breaking point far from its source. All that's left to come is the unravelling, the slow litany of pain, illness and death. We have surpassed our low peak and momentum's building as we roll downhill to the finish.

It's cold and my head is spinning. I should have eaten more, but the wine filled me up too much. My mouth is hanging open and my heart is thumping, something to do with blood sugar. Nothing is left of me but my name, and my name is false. I'm too insubstantial to connect with anyone else even if I had anyone around to connect with. I'm space-borne debris a billion miles from the next object, so far away that I can't be seen. I'm mouthing something like 'Fuck it, fuck it' and unbuttoning my shirt despite the cold, just because I want to feel something, anything, even if it's something less than pleasant from my cold universe. The wine has really kicked in and I'm breathing heavily. I stand, feel momentarily dizzy, steady myself with the chair. It's not cold enough. I sigh and make my way to the door, open it, stare out into the blackness of the garage. It's a long way from the sun this far out in space. My eyes are accustomed to the dark. The bars call to me. I stumble down the stairs and over to the bench. For a moment I lean there. 'Fuck' I say, or someone like me says. I could stop right here, collapse and go no further. And that would be it forever, no actions, no consequences, nothing else, but I'm not quite ready yet. I climb onto the bench and reach for the first bar.

My bare skin shudders in contact with the cold metal. I'm hand over hand, slowly then more quickly. I have done so much of this, across the full width of the garage and back to the middle. Then up. Tonight, for the first time, I will not stop until I have done all six frames. I go too fast. Fuck it. I screw my eyes up and slow down. My long body dangles into space as I go along, and up and down and to the next frame. The pain rises until it becomes a thing in itself, a fire burning at my limbs. *One, two, three, four... five*. My shoulders feel like they are pulling out of their sockets. Frame five, the bar less travelled. Dust falls into my eyes from the new section that I traverse, but it's climbers' chalk on my sweaty hands. The cold air eddies against the wetness of my chest and back. Sweat runs down my sides. It's too much. I swing up and latch my legs onto the bar. I think I say, 'Help me'. The bar digs into the flesh of my calves. All that remains is my thumping, thumping heart and the swooshing pulse of blood in my head. I am fully at the end of myself. God knows what time it is; time matters not when you are transfixed in the present by a giant spike. I can't get my breath back. I don't think about it. I don't want to think about anything ever again. I unwrap myself and lower my legs back down to be ready. I hear myself sigh, hand over hand and on to frame six, slower now, each move tearing at the sinew, gritting my teeth, across to the side of the garage, back to the centre, begging for mercy, for sweet deliverance, an end to all pain. Back to the centre, slower and slower with more time between each move, yet mediated by the need for haste. I can't hold on forever. I'm already past my limit and now I have to rise through the bars to the apex of the roof, pulling my dead weight upwards on arms that have to bend to drag me against gravity giant spans of impossible dimension. Oh god.

I can see the last goal, the two foot bar that makes the horizontal just beneath the point of the apex. My left hand catches a snag of weld and blood runs down my arm, mixing with the sweat. I wipe the hand on my hair as to regain the grip as I hold on with my right. I pull myself up for the last time...

I hang from the apex. My body falls away below me,

stretching out into space, drawing out under its own weight heavier and heavier, longer and thinner. My arms scream, but I must hold on. I hold or I fall. These are the options. The fall would break me, perhaps for good. The chattering in my head swirls into a rush that breaks like a wave, reforms and comes again, mixes with the agony in my arms and the tendons in my hands, down the stretch of my body to my feet however far below. *Hold on or fall.*

Morning comes by degrees. First is the intense dryness of dehydration sensed in the hours before dawn, the mind seeking ways to wake me to find water. Then there is the being awake and then asleep in quick succession, one and the other in alternation, but neither fully formed. Last there is gradual return of the self. The pain registers in the head and then elsewhere. It has been there so long through sleep that it has become the norm.

Light forms slowly in the apartment, grey then blue, then impossibly bright despite grey skies. I have lain down with my boots and trousers on, atop the sheets, dust dried with the sweat on my chest. It's hard even to sit up. The best I can do is to prop my head against the headboard. I don't remember anything. Not even my name. But that's okay because it comes to me carried in on the wind. 'John'. Yes, that will do for now. 'John.' More insistent now, telling me that this is how I will be known and how I shall be addressed. 'John.' Louder now to drive home the point: this is all you are and all you shall be. This is your lot and your destiny. 'JOHN!' Very loud, a call to duty, a reminder that there are consequences to a name that call you from your bed. 'John, for fuck's sake.'

I stand at the top of the stairs, bare-chested, looking down onto Bill just inside the garage door. A rare visit.

'John, I didn't think you were in.'

'I'm in.' Where else would I be?

'We're doing it tonight.'

JOHN

My building job in the East Midlands didn't last. Three weeks into the work I turned up to find a complete change of personnel. I was paid off. Seems that, now the groundwork had been done, the refitting had suddenly gone to a work gang from Eastern Europe. The old boys had already left, so that banjaxed any plans I might have had about following them on to their next job. More than that, the tiredness and futility of it all caught up with me the moment I walked off the site, so I hung around until the pub opened, ruffled through my cash and drank as much of it as I could fit in.

After the job was gone I was more at a loss than ever before. I sat in my house doing nothing. Stupidly, for those few weeks of work, I'd raised my expenditure in proportion to my incomings; probably more so. And you don't get any severance pay when there's no contract. One day I was working and the next I was staring at the walls. I eked out my money in quantities of small change. Economy packs of lasagne were now a luxury that I could only allow myself at weekends, though I soon lost track of when the weekends were. If I had any drink at all it was over-strength cider: the cheapest way to get drunk on a budget.

I knew I was coming to an end. Coming to an end reminds you how you came to begin, which led me again to things I didn't want to reconsider and visions I didn't want to re-see. It was obvious that my entire time on the run had been heading down a cul-de-sac. I was no further forward, only now broke. Not that that had stopped me spending what I'd got. I carried on until I had only a few pounds left. Even though I knew, on one level, that funds were finite, it had been so long since I'd actually had no money at all that I couldn't get my head around the concept until the last pan of dhal was running out.

The ad I put in the takeaway window said, 'House Clearance, Saturday. Everything to go at Knock-Down Prices.' Just three people turned up, even though I kept the door open all day. All three were more like vultures than bargain hunters. I sold my armchair and my mattress, my pots, pans and plates, my CD Radio and my few CDs, most of my clothes, my bed linen, my three books and the blue plastic basket that lived beneath the sink that held the cleaning things (along with the cleaning things). All that remained from my household things was an under blanket and my duvet without its cover, one melamine cup and a flower-patterned casserole dish that I couldn't even give away. I guessed that most of my things were destined for car boot sales. I made a grand total of forty-eight pounds and fifty-three pence, of which fourteen pounds went on one bottle of Burgundy which I drank from my melamine cup, propped up against the wall of the living room.

I stared blankly into infinite space. When the lights are off the partial darkness looks like it contains substance, a dark matter that inhabits the spaces between air molecules. It has a texture like smog and swirls into shapes that mimic the painful thoughts in your head.

I'd had my final notice on the house. I worked out how long the deposit would run in lieu of rent and that was tomorrow. I could have stayed on through the prolonged process of eviction but, despite all the things I am, I am not a cunt and I wasn't going to enjoy the benefit of facilities for which I hadn't paid.

There was nothing left in the gas meter and the house grew colder as the mid-winter frost worked its way through the walls towards me. I brought the duvet down from upstairs and wound it around me to keep warm. I had another thought and collected every last thing that I had and brought them through to the living room so we could all be together. There wasn't much: the travel bag that had once held all the money, a few clothes, my toothbrush and toothpaste, quarter of a bottle of shower gel and an unopened packet of condoms. I took the thirty odd pounds from my pocket and spread it on the floor. Even under the duvet my feet were growing cold, so I threw Enright's jacket over them and closed my eyes.

I've never been good at making decisions. Because of this I have become involved in unspeakable things. Sometimes, however, a decision is all that's left to you.

Where could I go? Nowhere without money or

someone to go *to*. Who could I go to? Dawn? No, because I'd already said goodbye for reasons of her own safety. Same for the thin remains of my own family. No one should become entangled with me again.

The wine finally kicked in and I started to reel, partly because I'd had nothing more than the last two slices of bread in the packet and partly because I was willing myself into oblivion. Then I did what I never do and started to retread the whole experience of The Route, the ups and the deep, deep downs, my relationship with Dawn, Gail, my lies and self-deceits, how the money made it all possible. I retraced my last trip, from London up the M1, through to the North east, seeing Dawn for the last time, the forlorn emptiness of the winter moors, the barn of lost souls, Motherwell and Bill.

And that was it. Bill was my last contact in an unconnected universe. Bill belonged to the world of The Route, a world of crime and casual violence. Whatever I was, Bill wasn't going to be fazed by that. Even so, what was my connection? Three years of drops and one night drinking with Bill when I was snowed-in and forced to stay over at his place. Sometimes there is only one choice or no choice at all and I never thought any further. My consciousness ran out and I slept.

I waited quietly a little way down the street. Motherwell at dusk, just like my last visit two years before, though this time without the van. It had taken me three buses and all the money I had left to get there. The middle leg from Nottingham had been interminable. I'd tried my best to look unsociable so that no one would sit next to me, but the coach had filled up and the one next to mine was the only seat left when the grandma got on with her four year old grandson, who was supposed to be sitting on her lap and for whom she had not bought a ticket to save money. He lolloped over me asleep most of the way, while she sat quiet and oblivious to my discomfort. It was so long since I had travelled and now it was travelling squashed up with inadequate leg room, elbow room and personal mental space. The boy dribbled and fidgeted with total abandon as if I was someone of complete familiarity.

The gates to the works were mostly shut. I'd remembered them open, with employees cars parked inside. It was too early for everyone to have gone home. And it was a Monday, so a working day. Still, Bill's company sign remained. I moved through the gates and into the yard.

How did I look with my long, unmanaged hair still bleached at the ends? An apparition. It was quite probable that Bill didn't even know I was still alive. That's how I left it last time: words unspoken.

The northern cold made me shrug. It was clear that there were was no one much around, but there was *someone*, as evinced by the silver Audi close to the shutter opening and light feeding from the upstairs. I tried not to be seen as I entered the building a bleached ghost. Light was dim from the first floor, but not so dim that I couldn't see that there were far fewer boxes of prophylactics on the shelves and some replaced with cartons of mobile phones with names like Samsung and Siemens. I smiled at the conjunction, even though my heart was thumping in my throat.

I slid past the shelves, a route familiar from the old days. A heavy-chested woman looked back at me from a calendar dated the year before last. No sounds of conversation from upstairs, so hopefully Bill was on his own. I climbed the stairs. By the time I reached the landing I had transformed from Wayne and back into John.

PREP

I wander up to the house. As ever, the grey sky walls me in from above. I am empty. Sometimes life contracts to a point that pins you in the moment.

Bill is in his office. Somehow it's clear that he's been awake for a long time. Still, he retains some measure of his stoic presence.

'All right, Bill?'

'All right, you got your stuff?'

'No, I'll fetch it.'

'Yeah, I want to go straight away.'

Even though I left the apartment minutes ago, it seems as if it hasn't been occupied for years. It has no semblance of home and so reverts to the nature of an uninhabited space as soon as I have left. I don't leave marks where I pass; they are left on me.

I collect my bag of things and return to the house. Bill's standing outside by the car. The chill damp of the air cools the skin in an unpleasant way, as if human beings were not designed for such conditions. The world cools you until you are frozen to the core and then you are cold at heart.

We drive up to the works in silence. Motherwell was always the northernmost point on The Route, rising up through the Midlands, the North East and the Borders, tipping over the top of the rollercoaster and cascading down the West. Now I am back and tipped over irretrievably into something else.

I feel like it's really late in the day to be T-cutting the van. It's something that could have been done weeks ago. We've known all along that a ghost of the company logo has remained from the time it was picked out along the van's flanks in adhesive letters. Bill sets me on to do it. It requires the old stepladder from the works, the bottle of T-Cut and two rags torn from an old T-shirt. It takes a lot of pressure and an inordinate amount of rubbing to remove the traces of adhesive. Worse than that, there's differential toning between where the letters have been stuck and the paintwork around them, which has oxidised to a matt grey rather than a clear white. It's clear that the whole of each side of the van will have to be cut back, otherwise the shiny patterns of refreshed paint might make it identifiable in comparison to others.

Bill has gone off to his office and I am left alone with this herculean task. The muscles in my arms and shoulders are aching like bastards from all the extra effort on bars last night, exactly the same muscles that are required to do this job. I will never make it through the day.

I give it half an hour and stand back to see what I've achieved. Fuck all. I guess don't have to do a perfect job, but it must be half way consistent. I get back on with it.

My muscles hurt immediately, though there is some advantage in that my 'on' rag is now fully saturated.

Euan arrives in his BM coupe. He has the false plates with him. He doesn't say anything, just commences to unscrew the old ones and change them over. That's him done. He stands back, brushes the dust from his hands and heads towards the warehouse.

Bill appears, 'Euan, give John a hand with the van.'

'You what?' There's an expression on Euan's face that I haven't seen before, something like when he fronted up with Ken, but without the confidence.

'Get to it man, John will never get it done on his own.'

Euan comes round to me, 'Pass me your cloth for a minute.'

'What?'

'Give me your fucking cloth.'

I pass him the one in my hand, which is the wet one. He goes around to the other side of the van with it. Now it is lost and I will have start again saturating my 'off' cloth. Both of us will have to get new cloths to clean off, so it's been a fucking waste of time all round. I know Euan will be doing the easy bits that he can reach and I'll have to follow up with the ladder, but that's the way life works with him.

Deep arrives when we are almost finished and does his little bit. Nevertheless, he stands back satisfied, as if he was there right from the beginning. Bill comes out to make sure that it's done to his satisfaction. It will be, because I've made sure there are no inconsistencies. Euan wasn't too happy about me going back over some of his bits, because he thought that it was good enough, but he's only a perfectionist when it comes to himself.

We sit in the secretaries' office waiting for Mal. It's mid afternoon in what already feels like a long day. The boys don't like waiting. Deep and Euan are set up for action and not prepared for quiet like me, accustomed as I am to empty existence. Bill is in his office doing something crucial regarding preparation. He's been in once to tell Euan to turn off the TV, which Euan didn't like. He literally bit his lip. I'm all too pleased: I don't think I could stand a whole evening of porn.

So, I sit with my two fretting colleagues wondering how it all comes to pass, that it's little to do with the decisions you make and more to do with the ones you've failed to make through a lack of conviction. And then I think that it's also true that, despite this sense of living in the moment, a conscious shutting out of what went before, you are still subject to it all whatever you do. And thus I sit here, waiting, and all because I used to drive up here on The Route and because I fell in with a bad crowd years ago, through a blend of moral cowardice and accepting a drink from a strange man in a pub when I should have known better. But then, it goes back further than that, to when I was a young graduate with prospects and I kind of squandered my birthright for nothing. Perhaps, regardless of this constant sense of being out of place, I have found my rightful place in the dregs with all these villains. And then, when I think of that, perhaps I am the worst of all, because I don't even have a higher goal. Mal wants to get hold of enough funds to win back his missus, Euan needs to supersede the disappointment of having failed to invest in the gym project. He wants to be a real geezer, maybe so that he can live up to his wife. Deep wants to re-house his sister Prema somewhere better than her current dump. For Bill, it's all about family. I don't have any excuses; I am just a mercenary.

There are many hours to go before we set out, long and empty and flavoured with discontent but, luckily, Bill appears with a pack of cards.

Mal arrives from the exhibition a little after four. He is cock-a-hoop.

'You should have seen it, man, it was packed with punters and me, just swanning around.'

'Did you unlock the window?' Bill asks.

'No, but I checked the window. I just slid down the stairs and no-one any wiser. The fucking catch was still unlocked from last time. What security?'

He reaches into the bag he's brought with him and pulls out a can of lager.

'No drink,' says Bill.

'What do you mean, man? I'm just having a wee snifter.'

'No drink.'

'You can't go on a job without a touch of Dutch courage.'

Bill rises from his seat and stands square on to Mal. It's enough.

'Ah fuck, man, fuck.' Mal is a schoolboy who has just been denied some treat. I expect him in the next instant to say something like 'it's so unfair'. Instead, he just sits down with his unopened can, deflated, 'Och, I'm fucking gasping.'

It's nearly seven. There's real tension now. I've noticed it building while we've been playing cards. It's volatile, a bubbling of noxious gasses that might ignite at any moment. Bill reaches into his pocket and brings out a couple of notes.

'Deep, go to the chippy and get us some fish and chips.'

'You what, Bill?'

'Get the lot of us something to eat.'

The boys perk up a little.

'Ah yes, Deep, get us a battered sausage and a large beans, will you?' says Mal.

'Aye, and I'll have a large doner meat and a garlic bread,' says Euan.

Bill pushes the notes into Deep's hand, 'Fish and chips, five times.'

I tidy up the remnants of the takeaway. The long day is

already a distant memory and instead has come the long night. Mal fills the office with fag smoke. Bill breathes heavily through his nose as if he were about to a face some powerful foe in the field. I am shaking, though I don't know if it's something to do with the after-effects of eating. We have played cards; Bill turns out to be best at that.

At twelve, those us who have need to change into our work clothes do so. Then we're all in our dark uniforms. We are soldiers sent out to perform a task. Is this how Enright felt? Did he sense duty or futility? Did he volunteer or was he conscripted? I get the thermal balaclavas out of my bag, hold one back and throw the others onto the table. Mal isn't quick enough and ends up with the one that looks like a pair of Y-fronts. Oh joy. Bill makes us put them on for a trial. Less like soldiers now and more like gangsters. This is the first time and they feel odd. The world is slightly dulled. We should have got used to them first. Mal smokes a tab through the hole in his. He looks a right tool. Deep takes his off in disgust and his hair sticks up.

'Load up,' says Bill.

We take our stuff to the van. Just when most people are safely tucked in for the night, we are setting off for work. We load in our bags, the pallet truck from the works, our two metal fabrications, Mal's tools and the short ladder. Bill makes me start up the van so that we can let it idle for a while to check that it's running okay.

The sound chatters off the walls, way too loud in the quietness of the night. There are no stars and the cold and damp has increased while we have been inside.

'Mobiles to silent,' says Bill to the boys. They all fumble around with their phones.

I feel weak and I have to drive. Euan and Deep are to ride in the back. Euan didn't like that.

There is nothing in my head, as if I have lost substance. I can't imagine anything outside this moment. I'm trying to remember how to drive a van. I've done it countless times, yet now I have to think through all the steps with conscious intent. I won't have the strength to turn the wheel.

If I have lost mass, then Bill has taken it on. He seems more solid than ever. There are no nerves with him, no doubts flickering through his eyes. He is just purpose. If it wasn't for that I might collapse where I stand and soak away like a spilled drink. But, whatever I've done, I've liked to do it right, so, one way or another, I'm going to manage. Mal gets into the cab and lights up another. He's smiling. It doesn't suit him. Bill pulls down the shutter at the back of the van and I manoeuvre it out of the yard. I wait in the street while he closes the yard gates. He climbs into the cab, forcing Mal to slide over towards me in far too intimate a manner, and I drive.

We rise to the topmost point and, after, it's all momentum carrying us inexorably towards our end.

WORK

I am at the top of the ladder, shaking. The window to the exhibition hall is locked. I try it again. It's locked. All four of the others are now out of the van, looking up at me as if I am a twat. I can read their looks regardless of the masks.

'What the fuck's the hold up?' says Mal.

I turn towards him and raise my palms in a 'what gives?' way. The boys say something to each other in loud whispers.

Mal comes to the foot of the ladder, 'Let me get at it.'

I climb down on unsteady legs. Mal is straight up the ladder as soon as I am clear. He pulls the window hard to no effect, as if I would make it up. For a moment he bows his head and curses thickly under his breath. He comes back down

'What?' says Bill.

Mal says nothing. He goes back to the van. The rest of us stand around like guests at a black-tie event who have been told it was fancy dress. I'm still shaking and all my momentum has dropped away.

Mal returns with a wrecking bar, his purposeful stride undermined by the impression that he's wearing underpants on his head. He scales the ladder and commences to feel along the bottom of the opening part of the window. Then he works the wedge end of the bar into the seam and waggles it to and fro to work it into the gap. We stand useless below.

The sound when the catch finally gives way is the loudest sound ever made by man, louder than a space shuttle launch or the Messines mines. I want to run far away, but Bill is pushing me towards the ladder, 'Go.'

This is crazy, there could be any number of guards scooting up inside right now to see what the noise is all about.

Mal has come back down the ladder, 'Go!'

I'm barely able to get up to the window. My legs don't want to work. I get to the top, pull open the broken window, heave myself over the threshold and drop quickly inside.

I am dead quiet. Who is coming? I get away from the window and go downstairs a way to hide in the shadows. But won't security come from downstairs? I go up the landing and listen. I go to the upstairs door and listen again. I put my ear to the door, but all I can hear is the swooshing of my own blood.

I keep listening, but the boys are exposed outside. It's a balance of risks. I go back to the window and wave for them to go. Euan draws the ladder away, rather too quickly, I think. I don't watch to see them leave, but return upstairs to listen again. The van rattles away into the distance. Shadows form in the stairwell and I am alone.

Sometime I will have to open the door and emerge into the exhibition space. I can't know if there is someone on the other side. It will only be a few seconds before I can get inside the offices via the next door down, but I will have stuck my head irrevocably above the parapet. If I am seen I am seen.

There's a time limit on this. We can't take all night over it. Waiting makes no difference. It's like being at a T junction on a bend: you can only see traffic when it comes round the corner. You have to leave when the bit that you can see is clear, as attempting to divine if there is anything coming out of sight is futile.

I seem to have stopped shaking. I open the door and step through...

As soon as I reach the office I flatten myself against the inside wall. I didn't detect anybody in the exhibition space, but I couldn't be sure. I have to wait again. It's very dark in here, lit only by screens. I cannot risk my headlight this time, though I have it in my pocket. If no one has seen me then I am safe here for a while: there is no camera.

I get accustomed to the dark. This time it's for real. It seems like a lifetime since I was last in this position, though it's only a matter of weeks. I think about the boys safe in the van in some back street and envy them. So far I'm the only one that's in trouble. Yet I have the doing and they have the waiting. Which is worse?

I cross to the connecting door and listen, not for too long. I push the handle gently and open the door slowly, as if it were made of fragile material. As soon as I am inside I hit the floor.

It's another office, like the last, but here there is a camera. This is what we've discussed all these times: what can it see. We think we know, but there's some guesswork – one of the variables.

I must crawl round, flat to the floor, following the perimeter. I crawl, sticking as close to the wall as possible. I slink round like fluid, a photocopier, a computer station, two desks. The next desk has no vanity board, so I crawl under its arch feeling smug. Pain stabs through the heel of my thumb. A fucking drawing pin! I pull it out and grimace, then suck at the blood. It won't stop coming. I stay under the desk going fuck, fuck, fuck in my head, but I have to be quiet, be sensible, steady down. I can't leave blood marks with my DNA. I peel off my green rubber glove and look at the dark spot. I have two spare gloves in my pocket. I get a fresh one and roll it on. Now the blood will stay inside. I breathe in once and recommence crawling...

The next room has no camera. So far I have heard nothing of security. I hope, I pray, that they are downstairs watching snooker. My phone vibrates against my leg. It's a text from Bill, *wots kepng u?* I send back a single exclamation mark: a dot with a pin.

I am at the last door. From here I have no option but to cross part of the exhibition space to the fire doors at the rear. If I am going to be caught on camera anytime, it will be now. This time I don't fuck about. Sometimes you need to act. I listen just long enough to be sure that there is no one close, open the door and go. I am steady; I walk purposefully like someone in security. If I run I might appear as a flash on a screen in the periphery of someone's vision in the security suite.

There is more light at the doors. The main lights in the hall are off, but some light is coming through the skylights, yellow light from the streets reflected off the clouds. I get out my screwdriver and tape. I look once more at the alarm sensors on the doors. This is our saving grace. There could have been any kind of concealed sensors, but these are just oblong plastic devices screwed to the frame, one at the top of each half of the split door. Better than that, the little metal plates on the doors that make the circuit are wider than the sensors themselves with the screws clearly visible. It's either a poor piece of design or the sensors replace older ones which were wider and the fitter simply couldn't be arsed to change them.

I pull off an appropriate length of tape and stick it temporarily to the back of my left glove. Then I start to unscrew one of the plates, a little at a time from both sides, finally holding the plate carefully while I finish taking out the screws. If it falls: game over. The screws come out. I take my length of tape and stick it to the back of the sensor, folding it around the ends and onto the plate so that the two are held together. I proceed to the next door.

When both are done I send Bill a text '*OK*' and wait for what could be five minutes or five days...

A soft knock. I push down on the bar to release one of the doors, slowly. Someone grabs it from the other side. I go to open the other. A little tearing sound. Shit, the plate's still stuck to the door. A hand is waiting to pull the door open. I grab it and hold it shut. Euan's masked face appears. I wave for him to stop and point at the sensor. A moment. I mouth the word 'knife'. He doesn't get it. Bill comes. His eyes say 'what?' I make two fingers into a knife shape and draw it back and forth. He gets it and pulls out his pocket knife, opens it and hands it to me. I work the blade behind the plate to loosen it from the door. It is stuck from time and nothing else. I refasten the tape and breathe again.

I hand signal. Bill and Euan hold the doors open and I tape all the way round the sensors so that the plates can't fall off. Then they're in: Bill, Deep and Euan.

Bill whispers, 'Got everything? Stun gun? Tape? Ammonia?'

What ammonia? This isn't something I've heard before. My two colleagues hold up their kit: the mobile phone stun gun, two rolls of duct tape, and two little lemon bottles the contents of which I guess you wouldn't want squeezing onto your pancakes. I shiver, but it's not the time for self-recrimination.

They go towards the steps that will take them down into the dungeon. As they stalk off, I can't help feeling that they are in their element. I look directly into Bill's eyes and he looks back and we wait like that: two masked statues dressed in black.

It takes our bouncer buddies the best part of a quarter of an hour. I dread to think what they're doing. I have too much imagination and I have seen too many unpleasant things. When you've seen the kinds of things I have, they remain ever present, just behind the thin veneer of everyday events. You could just turn one wrong corner and they could happen to you or to someone you care about. That's why I go ahead without anyone close.

In due course, they return. Bill's been getting more and more agitated, 'What took you so long?'

'We had a little trouble,' says Euan. One of his gloves is ripped.

'What trouble?'

'One of them didn't want to co-operate. We had to persuade him.'

I don't want to think about that. I block it out.

'What about the cameras?'

'They're off; we're all set.'

'Sure?'

'Sure.'

'Are there any more guards in the building?'

'They said no.'

'Deep, go and check the building.'

'They said NO.'

'Deep, go.'

Deep goes off.

'Euan, change your glove.'

Euan forces another green glove over the old one. I wish I'd thought of that. Blood is forming a dark stain beneath mine. It would congeal better if the air could get to it.

We open the doors wide. Bill has two small wooden wedges that we push in to hold them open. We can relax a little now that the cameras are off.'

'John, help Euan with the truck.'

The van is parked just beyond the fire escape. The fire doors open onto a small rectangular space protected by a strong tubular handrail and a flight of a ten to fifteen steps goes down to the right. We go straight to the van and collect the pallet truck. It's heavy, especially to carry up steps. We manhandle it though the door and place it on the floor.

'Let's go,' says Bill.

I now have time to take in the exhibition space once more, the furniture, the shelves of pottery, the scrap metal sculptures, in the centre the long jewellers' table taking centre stage. I think about the pretty lady jeweller with the long hair. Beyond, the gold and silver and gemstones grey in the shadows. We wheel our truck in the opposite direction.

There are six machines in the DVD exhibit, three for producing the discs *en masse* and three for making the glass masters. They come in different sizes. We are taking them all.

The smallest go first. Deep comes back just as we are

about to start. Apparently, there are no more guards in the building. I wheel the truck up, lower it to its lowest setting and activate the brake. Euan and Deep rock the machine sideways. This is what they are for. The machine is packed with mechanics and electronics and it's heavy. I push the truck under and they lower it down. Once it's on we push and pull and coax it to the fire exit. We drop it off and go back for the next.

Light falls softly through the roof windows. We work smoothly, ascending through the scale of machines as we've discussed, getting the technique right. We are demons with our masks on, in a cave of treasures. I am excited, exhilarated; all concerns except for the job in hand fall away. Each step brings us closer to our goal.

Euan stops and heads back towards the exit.

'Where you going?' says Bill.

'We need Mal, speed things up.'

Bill doesn't seem to think so, but Euan has already gone. The time spent fetching him is lost and we have to stand around, negating any advantages. Nevertheless, in the fullness of time we get the six machines lined up by the exit.

'Right, Mal.'

Mal has the inverter already crocodile-clipped to the battery. He lays out the long extension, up the steps while Deep brings the plasma cutter.

The bright light cuts through the rail quickly. It's good that this area is out of sight, but we have planned this. Bill draws on his thick gloves and holds the top rail as Mal makes a second cut. The metal glows red. Soon the rail is free and Bill carries it away. Mal moves onto the lower rail. Soon we have a gap opposite the doors. Bill looks at me. No words. I get down to the van, start it up and reverse it up slowly. Bill signals 'cut' when he thinks I'm in the right place.

Between us, we drag out the ramps we made and manoeuvre them between the gap at the top of the stairs and the load floor of the van. The angle plates that Bill has estimated by eye fit exactly flush with the concrete of the fire escape and the load floor of the van once we have fine tuned its position by pushing it back manually.

Endgame. We bring the machines down the ramps one by one on the pallet truck. With the heavier ones it's hard to hold them back against the gradient even with the truck's brakes activated. It was never designed for this steep a slope. Five down and one to go.

'Where's Mal?' says Bill.

I hadn't noticed he was gone.

'He's gone to look at the gems,' says Deep. 'He said he had to.'

'The cunt. He'd better not fuck this up.' Bill looks at the last machine, just visible inside the building. 'Let's get him.'

He's coming back just as we get back to the top, the stupid, pant-faced twat.

'There's someone in here,' he says.

'What are you talking about?'

'There's someone in here, some more folks.'

'Police?'

'No, I dinnae fucking know.'

I go with Bill, back into the hall. It's quiet then, no, a footfall, a scurrying in the shadows like rats in the attic. I think I see someone amongst the sculptures, then I'm not sure. I hear them; I don't know how many. They're talking. Talking about us? They must have got in through the fire escape when we were all preoccupied.

Bill moves forward, 'I'm going to find out what's...'

Euan comes up behind and grabs Bill by the arm. Bill swings round with his fist raised.

'No, Bill, fuck it. Let's get out of here.'

Bill's eyes are bright gemstones in the gloom. He shakes off Euan's hand. There's a moment, then he seems to settle, 'Right, let's get gone.'

I fear the men in the dark. Something is quite wrong. The last machine goes down the ramp in double-quick time even though it's the heaviest. Bill looks around him. Everywhere is danger.

'Come on,' says Euan.

We get the ramps and the rest of the kit back into the van. Euan and Deep stay in there with the machines. I climb into the cab and with Bill and Mal.

'Wait a minute,' I say.

I get out of the van and race back up the steps to the fire escape. I wrench at the tape on one of the sensors until the plate comes away. The alarm goes off instantly. Whoever's inside, whatever they're up to, they'd better act quickly.

Bill is beside me. He pulls the wedges from the doors and pushes them to. He looks at me. Between us we drive the wedges into the gaps at the bottom of the doors to effectively lock them shut, then back to the van.

It turns over lazily on the starter. There is hardly anything left in the battery. The plasma cutter has all but drained it. This is bad planning: we should have had a separate battery. The engine cranks over at a fraction of its usual speed, dying away. Then it catches, just. The engine spins into life. I gun it to make sure that it doesn't stall and head out.

The blue lights greet us as we get on to the main street. Mal rips his mask off just in time.

'Steady,' says Bill'

I'm steady, but I don't want to be. No crime works if you don't get away with it. The getaway is more important than the crime. The blue lights pass by on the other side of the road. I wait, expect, that they will stop, pause and turn round to come after us. I know it will happen. My heart beats like a steam hammer. Mal says something like 'fucking, fucking hell.' Another Police car passes us, and a fire engine. My wet hands slip around inside my rubber gloves. The blue lights recede in the door mirror. They don't stop; they don't turn around.

'Fuck it,' says Bill. 'We've done it.'

MONEY

We're in the Waverley celebrating. Bill has hired out the function room. It's full of people I don't know. I don't know if they know what we're celebrating. There's a buffet with sausage rolls, scotch pies and all that guff. I'm not hungry. I just want to drink. A lot. I've brought the van and Bill's brought the Audi, but we're getting a cab back. That's for sure.

I don't want to fall over too soon, so I'm drinking stout. It will save me eating later. People around me are smiling and having a laugh. Mal is pissed out of his head even though it's still early evening. He's already cornered me once and banged on about how it was certain he'd get his wife back now that he'd got some cash. I had mine yesterday, thirty-three thousand in bank notes. I put it straight into my travel bag. Something had changed and nothing. When I took my eyes away and looked around the apartment, it was as if I'd just set eyes on it for the first time. I stared back into the bag, with its tightly bound bundles of notes and felt my breathing rise and fall. I could cry, but not for joy. I stayed like this for some time before I was able to move.

Offloading the DVD machines went exactly according to plan. We never even removed them from the van, we just changed the plates back and headed out the day after the robbery. Only Bill and I went; only Bill knew the details. The place was on the north side of Glasgow, one of those small, corrugated industrial units exactly like the one from which we used to administer The Route. It made me shudder just to be there. We were met by a large, humourless man in his late forties with a gold earring. He didn't much like the look of me but, then, I'm just the driver and I don't figure in the niceties.

'Back it into the unit,' he said.

I backed the van completely inside and our host brought down the shutter. Our old unit in London was pristine and lovely, but this one reeked of something half recognisable and had detritus strewn everywhere. When I climbed out of the cab there were half a dozen more likely lads standing round looking assortedly bored, threatening or both – just like old times. How these deals are set up I don't know. Down here in the underworld it's a web of connections and rumours and reputations. Things go on without reference to the normal world. It wouldn't surprise me if everyone else knows what is going on at all times and I'm the only one in the dark.

Bill was already busy counting the money. I don't know how much the machines are worth on the legitimate market, or whether the bods were paying a premium to get hold of them anonymously, but there was a lot of money being handed over. I guess they'll be going on to various locations to churn out yet more fake DVDs for huge mark-ups. There must be a lot of money in it, because the guy in charge didn't seem bothered by what he was handing over, only that the machines were in tip-top condition and ready to go.

We didn't help with the unloading. The group just got to it with a portable platform on a scissor lift and had the lot away pronto. When we were done, the man shook Bill's hand and we went on our way. I was pleased to leave. Bill was obviously elated. All that anguish over the future of the house gone. He gets the king's cut of the proceeds. We soldiers all get the same. In spite of what it means, it's really not a life-changing sum for me. After we took the van back to the works, Bill divvied up my share straight away, as if he didn't want the burden of my part any more. I watched him as he was counting it out, knowing that my contract was up. Bill might not have thought it through as consciously as that, but that's what he felt. Why would he want someone like me close to his family? This business has always been a separate issue, so he's not going to want some reminder of it living in a grotto at the bottom of the garden. When it comes down to it, my tenure here has been an interlude and not a residency. That's why the money went straight into my bag and why I felt no satisfaction in it. When it comes to it, I turned up, prostituted all that was left of my thin morals and achieved nothing more than buying myself some more time on the run. When that's gone, I will be no better off, just further ahead in time and tides.

We have kept an eye on the news. There's been

something about the robbery, but nothing specific other than that there are a number of people 'helping the Police with their enquiries.' They haven't been to bother us. There won't be any forensics worth anything. Who could pick out the odd skin cell or eyelash from all the people that have been through the exhibition hall legitimately? We planned it well, we executed it well and now we're free, the last stage of any criminal plan: to get away with it. They may have caught whoever was fucking about in the dark when we left, but where are the machines? They've moved on too. What can the security guards say? Not too much, I guess. There's no connection with any of us, there's no fingerprints or conclusive CCTV and the false plates have gone into deep water.

I go up to the bar and get myself another pint of stout. Deep is there buying a lager.

'How's Prema?' I say.

'What?'

'How's Prema getting on?'

The look he gives me suggests that it is none of my business, 'Yeah, all right, getting a new place.' Then he turns away and takes his drink with him, back to a group of lads of a similar age who seem to be having a great time. I hear Mal gurning away in the distance. I've had enough of his voice. I sit down with my pint and have a look at it. I am alone. I keep on feeling angry with myself, which carries on until I'm worn down, worn away to a stub. There is nothing. There is nowhere to go.

I could go anywhere with my money that doesn't require a passport, but I've already been anywhere. I spent two years doing that and it's nowhere.

This is the end of me. I will never again feel the finer emotions, scale heights, hold high hopes, love on a summer's day, wake with anything in my heart. There will be no love poems or letters written in passion. There will be no photographs to recall special moments. Whatever happens in the formless void of my future, I will not register or plant seeds to propagate in anybody's memory. I am forgotten. All that I have achieved in my sorry life is to have undermined and devalued myself at every step. I drain the pint I have just started.

The room is a buzz of people who know where they belong. I've finished with the Guinness and moved on to spirits, even though I know it will be my downfall. I don't care. Tomorrow I will gather my few things and leave. I won't say goodbye. That would be best. When I think, my thoughts go nowhere. I've blanked out my past for so long that it leaves cold trails in my mind. Yes, it's a lie. You can't give up the past, because you are the sum total of what's happened to you, and now I have four months of new past to contend with. What it all adds up to doesn't bear consideration.

Some old geezers are chatting to Bill. There's a real air of celebration. It goes on over there. I wonder if Justine would have been allowed to come if she wasn't working late. I check the time. It's not long past eight and I'm already spinning. Perhaps I should just go.

It takes me a few minutes to find my feet. I wait until Bill is free. He's popular tonight, so it takes a while. When I get my chance I buttonhole him.

'Bill, I'm going.'

'Are you? Taxi's not coming 'til twelve.'

'No, I'm bushed.' He looks a little disappointed, but only, I think, because it might be something of a snub to his party preparations.

'Boys are happy, anyway,' I say by way of compensation.

'Yeah.'

'Where's Euan? I haven't seen him all evening.'

'No, he came early to collect his money and just fucked off.'

'Perhaps he went to see his mate.' I don't know why I say it.

'What mate?'

'The one he was talking to the other night in Starz. They were really engrossed, so I didn't bother them.'

Bill looks deep and hard, right into my soul. The words come slowly and powerfully. They take me aback, 'WHAT MATE?'

'Er, I don't know, short guy, black hair, big moustache.'

'That's Osman.'

CONTRACTS

The van clatters through the dark. I am far too drunk to be driving, but I have to. I am all adrenaline. It's too far and the van is too slow. Bill has the Audi. I was going to go with him until I remembered and broke off without a word, no time for explanations, no minutes, no seconds.

It's clear what's happened: Euan's sold us out. I can only guess when that happened, sometime after our visit to Ken over the trainer deal. Sometime later Euan must have paid a visit to the mysterious Dougie. Dougie, they said, was something to do with Osman. Osman must have made Euan an offer. Whoever else was in the exhibition hall with us was sent by Osman. To steal the jewels? Probably. Who knows? I guess the Police will be asking them that.

They don't just kill you. That's the thing. The van is ludicrously slow. I scream it though the gears to the rev limiter. It's not designed for speed. My reactions aren't what they should be, what with all the alcohol swimming around my blood stream. 'Come on, you fucking cunt, please.' I feel tears in my eyes: frustration. Bill has gone with Deep in the Audi. Mal was too far gone for anything. 'Justine,' said Bill. Osman will want revenge. It's all about territory; it's all about business interests.

Who were the men we shut in the hall? Hired hands? Close associates? Family? Does it matter? Bill went white. 'Justine,' he said. We gathered up Deep and went for Mal, but he was just a happy sap with a whisky in his hand who didn't recognise the alarm in Bill, a man who is never alarmed. We headed quickly to the car. 'Thank God Lauren's at Kirsty's.' Yes, thank God, but she's not is she? It's the night of the party and Bill doesn't know about it, she's at home waiting for the cab that's taking them to the party: it's our secret.

So I stopped right there, turned and headed for the van. No time for words.

There is too much traffic. I don't know how much time matters, but every second is too long. I go through the red lights. *Lauren*. The night is wet and cold and I have the window open, seeing those everyday people on their everyday evenings going about their business. I crash past them in my vehicle. It's so hard and it's not just the alcohol: that has somehow worn off to be replaced by a terrible dread. I leave the town and drive out into darkness. I overtake a saloon, but the van is not fast enough. An oncoming car steers into the verge and I just make it past, to the sound of angry horns. Closer, all my concentration forwards, reeling in the distance.

I turn into the entrance to the house. The van strikes one of the gateposts and I lose control, careering into the front of the garage and coming to a sudden halt. I'm out. I don't turn off the engine, I'm just out and headlong up the drive to the house. I see the shit-heap hatchback parked outside. I see the door, but it's not right. There is a large hole where the handle used to be. I get my knife from my pocket and bring out the blade. The door opens. I raise my knife. There is a figure in the doorway. He points his stick at me. I feel it before I hear it, points of pain. Yet it doesn't really hurt, it's more like a surprise. There's a spread to it, from my left shoulder and down my arm and upwards to my neck. Something pings into my forehead above the eye, another closer to my tear duct and all that I can think of is that he's fired too early, that there's too much spread from a sawn-off at this range. I don't stop. I can't stop. I see him break the gun and the two spent shells spitting out the back. He reaches into the pocket of his coat and presses two fresh cartridges into the breach, but he's too late. I go straight through him and we clatter backwards through the doors together. He goes over and the gun bounces down the hall. He comes to a rest. I go on, sliding on the laminate until I hit the telephone stand.

Somewhere there is screaming, somewhere far off, but close at heart. I try to get up, but slip on my own blood. The gun man is up and heading past me down the hall. I grab him by the trouser leg. He turns and stamps on my back. The screaming has stopped. It came from upstairs. I lunge out from the wall and catch his leg again. This time he goes down with a thud, but turns quickly and pushes down ready to get up. I drag myself onto my feet and onto him. He punches me in the face with an iron hand. My nose cracks. My eyes flash white light. When it clears I am on my back again and he is half way up. Blood is running into my eye. He grinds his hand into my shattered nose and I scream blue murder. He's on his feet. He kicks me full force in the side of the head. I look. He is almost at his gun. I push myself up, onto my knees, towards him. I see my knife by the wall. He gathers up his gun and brings it up to bear. I drive the knife upwards through the base of his jaw. It strikes his palate and breaks through. He looks surprised and yelps, but I have pinned his tongue. The blade snaps from the handle. He falls backwards onto the laminate and clutches at his throat. Crimson bubbles froth at his lips.

I am fast upstairs. Blood flows into my eye. I have never been upstairs before. Each instant's so long that I can take in the family knick-knacks and the prints Justine has picked out to adorn the walls. I don't know where Lauren's room would be, but there is a noise and motion behind an open door.

He sees me straight away, a small man with a face like a snarling dog. It is Lauren's room. She is on her bed. The dress she bought for the party is torn around her waist. There is blood. She doesn't move. They don't just kill you. The small man grabs my neck and stabs me in the chest. I look down, strike his hand from the hilt and drag the point from where it has stuck vertically between my ribs. It drops from my hand. He punches me first in the throat and then in the face and I stagger back. He brings his arm back for another. I fall forwards and embrace him. I cannot hold him. He is like a wild animal, turning and writhing and striking out. He gets away and I hold his arm. I push his face, but he bites through the heel of my thumb. Lauren lies still on the bed, her mouth open. *You fucking, fucking, fucking, fucking cunt. You fucking, fucking, fucking, fucking cunt.* I hold him again and he explodes out, catching my nose. He punches again, but I nod my head and he hits me in the forehead hard. It hurts him more than it hurts me. I grab the wrist and pull him towards me. A spray of spit mists me like the shotgun pellets earlier. I push him down and my hand closes round his throat. He squirms. I go down with him and try to hold him fast. I wrap my legs around him as he writhes in my grasp. I lean into him. My steel hand which has held me aloft all these times in the garage grips his windpipe. All my forgotten, subordinated passion arrives in a dam-burst rush and engulfs me, rising in the vale and obliterating everything. This is all that's left, a single action to stop him in his task. I crush the fucker beneath my fingers as he writhes and beats and punishes me with his fists, his elbows, his nodding, ballcock head bouncing on the carpet. I press him into himself with thoughtless, unrelenting pressure like a steam cylinder, rising without fall. Blood seethes between my clenched teeth. I press him into the floor. Something cracks beneath my fingers. I press on and extinguish his purpose... but not his life. Even now, I draw back from that. His eyes roll up into his head; he goes limp; his nodding stops.

I disentangle from him and gather myself onto all

fours. A string of blood and mucus reaches from my mouth to the floor and begins to form a stain. I spit it out. I feel the pain in my shoulder now. I am spent. There is nothing left. I roll onto my back by the bed. My foe wheezes gently beside me, unconscious. Lauren makes a sound, a low sound: 'John?' I'm not sure if I really hear it or whether it is something that I have made up because I want to hear it. Then, a pale, smooth hand lolls from the bed. I am stuck to the floor. I reach up and fold her hand in mine. 'John,' she says.

I am far, far, far, far gone... but I am not yet lost.

Printed in Great Britain
by Amazon

36109977R00126